"I'm your man," he promised

Taylor simply smiled at him. Even the torrential downpour didn't distract him. She'd gone only about three steps toward the beach bungalow when Dev's arm looped around her, turning her to face him. Then he was kissing her mindless while the warm rains drenched them. Lightning crackled nearby, and they ran inside for cover.

Impatience gouged at her, impatience to feel him hard and hot in her hand. Impatience to have him hard and hot inside her.

He hooked his fingers in the sides of her bikini bottom and pulled it down slowly over her thighs. Her muscles went weak and she sagged backward into the macramé hammock chair hanging from the ceiling. His eyes looked black, the pupils dilated with desire. He got down on his knees in front of her as she slid to the edge of the chair and hooked her feet over his shoulders. Before she could say anything, he leaned in and put his mouth against her where she was slick and hot.

"You certainly are..." was all she could manage as a response. She let out a soft cry as he went to work with his talented tongue—teasing her, tormenting her in the way that after mere days he'd learned she liked best.

Dear Reader,

All the books in the UNDER THE COVERS trilogy were great fun to write, but *Slippery When Wet* was undoubtedly the best. You see, I put together the opening chapters while sitting on a beach in Cozumel, soaking up sun and listening to the waves (don't ask if I dropped top—I'll never tell). My husband and I took our honeymoon in Mexico, and it's been a special place for me ever since. I loved the idea of a holiday fling, of lovers exploring the tropics...and each other. As for the things you can get away with doing at a beach resort, well, let's just say the book let me unleash my creativity.

It's a summertime book designed to be read on the beach. Still, we can't always be on vacation. If you wind up reading it at home, I hope you still get the scent of cocoa butter and the feel of sand between your toes. Close your eyes and let me take you where the tropical breezes blow. Drop me a line at kristinhardy@earthlink.net and tell me what you think. Or visit my Web site at www.kristinhardy.com for contests, e-mail threads between characters in my books, recipes and updates on my recent and upcoming releases.

Have fun,

Kristin Hardy

Books by Kristin Hardy

HARLEQUIN BLAZE
44—MY SEXIEST MISTAKE
78—SCORING*
86—AS BAD AS CAN BE*

*Under the Covers miniseries

SLIPPERY WHEN WET

Kristin Hardy

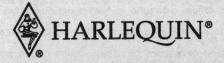

HARLEQUIN®

TORONTO • NEW YORK • LONDON
AMSTERDAM • PARIS • SYDNEY • HAMBURG
STOCKHOLM • ATHENS • TOKYO • MILAN • MADRID
PRAGUE • WARSAW • BUDAPEST • AUCKLAND

To Holly, who knows why,
and
to Stephen, for being my rock.

ISBN 0-373-79098-8

SLIPPERY WHEN WET

Copyright © 2003 by Kristin Lewotsky.

Prologue

ELIOT HAD GOTTEN IT WRONG. April wasn't the cruelest month, thought Taylor DeWitt as the needle sharp bits of ice whirled down in her face, February was. Late February, more precisely, the month of bone-chilling sleet, the month when winter seemed endless, the month of her worst ordeals.

On the other hand, February had been the month she'd gained her freedom, the month she'd found her strength, the month she'd launched her business three years before. An uncommonly successful launch, she thought, shivering at the edge of the crosswalk in the biting wind that blew in off Baltimore's Inner Harbor and plastered her chin-length blond hair down to her head. The city's picturesque Chesapeake Bay location lost some of its charm in winter. Farther inland, powdery snow might blanket the rolling Maryland countryside, but here in Baltimore the winters were just icy, clammy and bleak, making people eager to go somewhere warm.

Small wonder then that February was the busiest time in the local travel industry, especially for an agency that specialized in tropical getaways the way hers did. Or had up to now, she thought balefully. She scowled at the scaffolding and construction barriers surrounding the skyscraper that housed her office. Being downtown kept her close to her corporate clients while bringing her walk-in business from the shopping and conference area. The location had been pure gold for her, but for months now, the loss of business due to construction had her company teetering on financial worry. Meanwhile, Alan Champlin of Champlin Travel kept hanging around to tempt her with flattery and a juicy buyout offer.

Another blast of icy wind whisked up under her coat as she crossed with the light and she gave a heartfelt curse. Thank God she was headed south soon. If construction was going to have her offices closed anyway, it only made sense. Her agents could still work at home. Taylor had warmer plans: two weeks of reviewing properties in the Caribbean, and then a few precious days for herself in Mexico.

She worked her way around the pedestrian detour that led to her office. The agency had only just begun making a comfortable profit the year before. She had a bit of a cushion from that and from the modest trust fund she'd used to launch the venture, but no firm could sustain such a revenue hit month after month. Four weeks, she reminded herself. In four weeks it would be done.

Or so the landlord had promised.

Despite the financial woes that dogged her, Taylor couldn't help smiling at the gold palm trees stenciled on the glass, the curling letters that spelled out DeWitt Travel. The business was hers, and she'd made a success of it, even with her current challenges. No way was she going to sell out to some mall chain. The chime jingled as she pushed open the door.

"Hi, Allie," she said to the receptionist, who sat behind her modular breakfront. "Did I get any messages while…"

"That's a crock," a voice said angrily. A male voice. "I bought the insurance, I did everything I was supposed to. Don't tell me it's no good."

Taylor looked over the ivy-topped barrier behind the receptionist. Whoever he was, he was tall enough for her to see his tousled light brown hair, not to mention a not-inconsiderable pair of shoulders clad in a dark blue parka.

"You need to fix it. Now." The words held the snap of ire and command. Taylor stepped swiftly into the office area.

He stood in front of Glynnis's desk. Glynnis was her newbie agent, who looked half alarmed, half mesmerized. All Taylor could see was faded jeans, heavy work boots, and the parka.

"Is there a problem here?" she asked in the calm, reasonable voice she'd developed to soothe even the crankiest customers.

He spun around to look at her and she understood the expression on Glynnis's face. He was tall. He was intimidating. He was obviously angry.

And he was undeniably gorgeous.

It took a conscious effort of will to remain cool. Cool, she found, was the best way of defusing anyone's anger. Except Bennett, who'd only ever gotten angrier, but he was only a dark memory.

This one had the carved cheekbones and strong chin of a Viking, and the menacing Viking had only fury in his eyes. His jawline might have been as taut as it looked, or maybe it was just because it was currently clenched in anger. She could imagine him clad in leather and fur, striding ashore from his galley to lay waste to a helpless town. His eyes, though, surprised her. Deep set and long lashed, they were a sea-green.

And currently narrowed in irritation.

"A problem? I'll tell you what the problem is. I bought travel insurance nine months ago when I booked this trip. Now I need to cancel and your agent is telling me that I can't."

"We can cancel it, sir. We just can't get you your money back." Glynnis looked at her helplessly. "He got the basic insurance package."

"Let me see." Taylor reached out for the policy. "This is trip interruption insurance. It's standard. Covers family death or hospitalization. Why are you canceling, Mr...."

"Carson. Dev Carson." His words were clipped. "The trip was a honeymoon. The wedding's been called off."

Wedded bliss wasn't for everyone, that much she knew from bitter personal experience. "I'm sorry to hear that."

"Don't be," he said shortly.

"Yes, well..." She scanned the insurance contract but she already knew the terms by heart. "Unfortunately, this policy doesn't cover your reason for cancellation."

"Then why do you sell it?"

She needed to concentrate on the discussion, not on the alarmingly fascinating angles and planes of his face. "It covers what most people need," Taylor said automatically. "On occasion, when we know people's plans call for something more comprehensive, we have that as well."

"It's not like I planned to call off my wedding. I didn't get a detailed explanation of the coverage choices. Under the circumstances, I think I should get my money back.''

''I'm sorry, Mr. Carson. There's nothing I can do. If the trip were just a couple of days perhaps we could work something out, but this is—'' she scanned his file ''—three weeks. We simply can't swing it, especially since you're scheduled to leave in four days.'' Especially now, when the company was as cash poor as it could be.

His brows lowered. ''Do you think I can afford to throw away that kind of money on nothing?''

''Perhaps you could still go. We could try to get the tour company to allow you to substitute companions. Maybe you could take a friend.''

''I'm not feeling like company at the moment,'' he snapped. Just for a moment, an emotion other than anger flared in those sea-colored eyes. ''Look, I bought the insurance I was offered. What are you going to do to make good on it?'' he asked with an edge to his voice.

It was Taylor's turn to bristle. ''Let's not get personal about this.''

''Oh, but it is personal, Ms. DeWitt,'' he said silkily, reading her name off her badge. ''My fiancée and I chose a destination—and insurance—based on your agency's recommendation. You look like the sort of person who believes in standing behind her business.''

Those extraordinary eyes held steady on hers. Guilt pricked at her. If times had been better, she'd probably have offered to make good on his trip. But times weren't good, Champlin was stalking her agency, and taking an $8,000 hit was simply out of the question.

''I'm sorry, Mr. Carson. I'll check into whether any

of the resorts or the tour company will give you a break. I warn you, though, at this point it's unlikely.''

''What's unlikely is that I or anyone I know will use your agency again,'' he said tightly.

''I'd urge you to reconsider taking the trip. Cozumel is lovely this time of year. I'll be down there myself soon on business.''

''Yeah? Well, I hope you make a better choice of travel agencies than I did,'' he said cuttingly and stalked out, letting in a blast of cold, damp air.

1

Exotic birds hooted as Taylor threaded her way along the flagstone path that wove through the lush Mexican jungle of the Iberonova resort, a straw bag slung over her shoulder. To either side of the central sweep of jungle lay the brightly colored stucco huts that housed the hundreds of guests, but a person would never know it. Walking down the winding path, watching monkeys swing overhead, Taylor might have been deep in the Yucatan jungle. A trio of rust-colored birds with nodding topknots on their heads stared at her as she walked by. The enormous, intricately carved stone medallion that leaned against a tree trunk off the path looked Mayan, as though she were approaching the ancient jungle city of Chichen Itza.

She emerged from the trees at the curving edge of an enormous free-form pool. Palm trees and brightly colored umbrellas shaded the guests who sprawled on lounges, dozing or reading or sipping fancy drinks from the swim-up pool bar. At the center of the pool, a stone fountain sprayed droplets of water that glittered in the sun. Cocoa butter scented the air.

And she was warm, warm, warm. No coats, no sleet, no shivering. A sarong and a bikini were all she needed, for the air was soft and hot as a lover's touch.

Taylor skirted the pool, heading toward the beach.

Ahead, a short stone walkway leading to the sand was lined with parallel walls of warm golden stone that rose higher than a man's head. On their inner surfaces, a series of primitively carved stone faces with Mayan features stared impassively at one another. A young girl turned a porcelain knob as Taylor passed and water gushed out of the stone lips and out of the fluted funnels below them. The guest showers, Taylor realized. Leave it to the Iberonova to turn even the prosaic into atmospheric whimsy. Then she looked through the showers at the vista beyond and caught her breath.

Ahead of her, curving palm trees framed the view of an ocean that stretched out an impossible shade of aqua, darkening to indigo on the horizon. A white catamaran with a sail banded in turquoise, blue-green, and magenta glided over the waves. Palm-thatched palapas dotted the beach like giant parasols, guests stretched out beneath them on sun couches. And the waves whispered.

She couldn't stop the smile.

For two weeks, she'd been hopping from island to island, resort to resort, sometimes three or four properties in a day. Every night, she was somewhere different, never anywhere long enough to unpack, let alone relax. It hadn't been about relaxing, though. It had been about work. Admittedly, work she enjoyed, but work nevertheless.

This, though, this was her time. Seven precious days to herself, to sleep in until noon, to read, to lie on the beach. To do absolutely nothing that she didn't want to do. She picked up her straw bag and started down the broad beach.

The sand was hot on her feet, the sun warmed her

shoulders and made her glad of her dark glasses. As she walked past the sun worshippers, she relaxed to hear the mix of languages. No Texas twangs or Southern drawls or nasal Yankee accents talking about PTA meetings and yesterday's big game here. The mix of French, Italian, German, and Spanish danced into her ears. Perhaps they were talking about the banal, but with the musical flow of syllables, it hardly mattered. The English she heard was from other shores—British, Australian, New Zealander. Americans were outside the norm here.

Which was probably just as well, considering the fact that most of the European and South American women matter-of-factly dropped top when they hit the beach. Taylor set her straw bag in the shade of a palapa, pulling over a sun couch. A beautiful Hispanic woman walked toward her, breasts standing out proud and high and completely bare. Taylor smiled to think how the vice president of the Rotary Club and his wife would have reacted to the sight. Probably just as well that she'd booked them to Fort Lauderdale.

She untied her sarong and spread her towel out on the lounger. For a moment, she stared at it, then she moved it back out into the sun. Just for a little while, she'd give herself the luxury of baking in the heat, before she yielded to reason and shifted into the shade.

Lying back on her couch, she sighed in pure bliss, listening to the soft rush of the waves, the breeze whispering through the palm fronds of the palapa. Reaching into her bag, she rummaged for the bottle of sunblock. With her brown eyes, she was the rare blonde who took to the sun readily, but it still paid to be careful in the tropics. She'd seen the lobster-red tourists and didn't want to be one.

She spread sunblock along her legs, idly watching a pair of topless women walking up the beach. What must it feel like to have the sun warm your bare breasts, skin that hadn't felt the caress of the sun in years, if ever?

It was a surprisingly enticing notion, she thought as she smoothed the coconut-scented lotion along her arms. Intriguing.

Tempting.

A woman on a sun couch nearby chattered something in what sounded like Italian to her male companion and turned to lie on her back. He made a pretend grab for one of her breasts and she batted his hands away laughingly.

Like night and day compared to what she'd known, Taylor thought, remembering her ex-husband Bennett, who'd had a positive aversion to sexually assertive women.

At least when the woman in question was his wife.

Taylor shook her head as she spread sunblock on her neck and chest. The past was the past. She wasn't the woman he'd cheated on, the demoralized mouse that he'd bullied into submission anymore. She'd ignored Bennett's rants and forced through the divorce. So what if marriage was just one more thing she hadn't finished? She'd been so focused on living down her family reputation as a quitter that she'd stayed in the marriage long after she'd realized it was toxic. Some things weren't meant to be finished. It was just as well that she'd gotten on with her life.

But had she? Taylor set the bottle in the sand. Until Bennett, she'd been quick to have a good time, quick to be outrageous. Before she'd quit college to marry him, those were the qualities—her sexiness, her wildness—that had drawn him. Then it had all come to a screeching halt. Since the divorce, since she'd gotten free of him, she'd rebuilt her self-esteem. She'd thrown herself into work and made a success of herself. It gave her pride. On the other hand, it had also taken all of her time and energy, leaving none for her private life.

No more, she thought in a sudden surge of recklessness. It was time to do something outrageous, time to live life like the old Taylor. After all, she *was* on vacation.

The Italian woman gave a magnificent roar of laughter, propping herself up on her elbows and giving her mane of hair a shake. Taylor lay back and closed her eyes. How Bennett would have hated the very idea of women sitting topless on a beach, though that wouldn't have stopped him from leering. And the very idea of Taylor doing anything so brazen, well, it would have given him a stroke.

A rush of daring whisked through her. Taylor's eyes opened and a slow smile spread across her face. Why shouldn't she? It wasn't as if anyone knew her here. She was thousands of miles from home. Going topless here was hardly outré—it was accepted. And wouldn't it feel marvelous, she thought as the sun soaked into her bones. Wouldn't it be amazing to be so free?

Before she could change her mind, she sat up and reached back to unhook her bikini top, shrugging so that the shoulder straps fell down to dangle against her arms. She took a deep breath, for courage. And then it was off and her breasts were swaying free.

The skies didn't part with lightning to strike her. The nattily attired resort security guard didn't swoop down in agitation. Basically, no one noticed.

Except her.

It was the breeze that surprised her most of all, the feel of air whispering lightly over skin unaccustomed to its touch. She felt wonderfully decadent and yet somehow at ease. The sun was like a warm kiss, making her laugh even as she resisted the urge to glance down to see if her nipples were hard. No one would notice if they were, she reminded herself, there were plenty of others around to look at. Closing her eyes, she lay back and basked in the heat.

Moments later, visions of sunburn and melanoma chasing through her head, she groped for the bottle of sunblock. Skin that hadn't seen the sun since she'd been a toddler—if even then—needed all the protection it could get. Leaning back on one elbow, she used the other hand to rub the lotion into her breast. She wouldn't feel bashful about touching herself, she told herself sternly. It was skin like any other on her body. She just needed to protect it, that was all. And yet the feel of her lotion-slicked palm rubbing over her nipple sent a surprising jolt through her system, making her yearn for more.

Now there was a sad statement on her nonexistent love live, if just putting sunblock on her breasts could turn her on. Of course, there really hadn't been anyone since Bennett. She'd focused on everything but her needs for far too long, Taylor realized suddenly.

Closing her eyes and settling back, she relaxed. What a person could do with a lover in the tropics. The sunlight shone red-orange through her lids. How would it be to have a man's hand stroking the sunblock on her body slowly, teasingly, the delicious friction of skin against skin bringing her to arousal? Her imagination painted them naked on a deserted beach, immersed in the feel of each other's bodies. Alone but for sun and sand, they reached for abandonment and beyond. His hand slid down over her breasts, across her belly, touching her the way she hadn't been touched in so long. The caress moved to her hips, up her thighs, slipping into the slick—

"Careful you don't get burned there. That skin's awfully pale," said a voice.

A male voice. A voice that was vaguely familiar, she thought with the first glimmer of uneasiness. The red haze of the sun on her eyelids had darkened, as though someone were casting a shadow over her. She opened her eyes.

And saw Dev Carson grinning down at her.

2

EMBARRASSMENT, COMPLETE, paralyzing embarrassment. No, it was worse than embarrassment, worse than mortification. Words didn't exist for how she felt just then.

"You'd better try some more sunblock on your face. It's looking pretty red," he said, not even trying to cover up the amusement in his voice. Oh, no, he was enjoying his moment fully.

It was a good thing one of them was.

Taylor reached out for her bikini top, her sarong, anything to cover up her bare breasts from his all-too-knowing eyes.

"Looking for this?" He held out her bikini top and grinned. "I don't know, pale skin like yours, you really ought to be more careful of the sun."

She refused to make a grab for the top. Instead she flipped over to lie on her stomach, her face flaming. What was he doing here? she thought wildly. According to the papers she'd seen, he should have been back in Baltimore long since. Maybe if she pretended she couldn't see him, he'd go away. Except that she hadn't put any sunblock on her back and already she could feel the sun's heat soaking in.

And he showed no signs of leaving. Instead he crouched down by her lounger, treating her to an up close view of a truly amazing set of six-pack abs.

What she could see of the rest of him looked even better. Great, she was half-naked in front of a stranger and here she was salivating over the way his biceps flowed up into the smooth spheres of his shoulders. Half of her, anyway. The other half was hoping for the sand to open up and swallow her.

Relax, Taylor, she told herself. Humiliation was rarely fatal, and if Mr. Hunka Hunka Burnin' Love was having a bit of fun at her expense, he probably thought she had it coming. Play it cool, that was the thing to do. The beach was full of beautiful women. When the entertainment value wore off, he'd probably go about his business. "I see you decided to take my advice, Mr. Carson, and have a vacation," she said, trying for her dry, customer relations voice, resisting the urge to ask what the hell he was still doing there.

As though he'd read her mind, he gave a slight smile. "Glynnis sweet-talked the tour company into giving me an extra week since it was only one person. You know, extenuating circumstances and all. I figured lying on the beach for a while and enjoying the—" he paused and looked her over "—scenery would be good for me."

"And has it been?"

His grin widened. "Ask me in a little while."

"So you came down alone?"

Dev nodded. "That's why I was so pleased to see you here." Pleased didn't begin to cover it. When he'd first seen her walk onto the beach, long and lovely in her copper-colored sarong, he'd thought he was seeing things. Back in Baltimore, still sporting fresh wounds to his pride, he'd been irritated by her cool attitude, frustrated by the news that his insurance was next to useless, and furious that she was willing to do little or nothing to help resolve the situation. But through it all, he hadn't been able to entirely ignore that swing of blond hair, those dark eyes, that hint of a dip in her lower lip that made that wide, tempting mouth look like she was perpetually prepared to kiss someone.

And she'd stayed on his mind.

She'd mentioned a business trip to the Caribbean, he'd remembered. Somehow, finding her sprawled on the beach had made him pretty certain that she was finishing up with a vacation of her own. As for Dev, he'd come south with one objective in mind: to find a pretty *señorita* to drive all memories of his failed engagement out of his mind. And if that *señorita* proved to be a *gringo* who'd refused to give him a refund, it would be all the sweeter. He'd watched her untie her sarong and wondered how she would undress for a lover. He'd seen her spread on the sunscreen and wondered how it would feel to touch her smooth skin.

And then she'd stripped off her top and his tongue had just about fallen out of his mouth. Paradoxically, some vestige of the gentleman in him had kept him focusing on her face, not her breasts, even when he'd approached. He didn't need to cop a sly peek. He knew he'd be able to look at his leisure, and soon.

He'd already decided he was going to seduce her.

Part of him was shaking his head wryly that the one woman who wouldn't get out of his head right now was the same woman who'd gotten under his skin in Baltimore. Then again, if it hadn't been for her refusal, he wouldn't be here on vacation. That didn't mean he wasn't still just a bit annoyed.

Now he looked at the downy hairs at the small of her back, on skin pinkening in the tropical sun. "You're going to get yourself a burn there if you don't get some sunscreen on. I'll help if you like." He picked up the bottle, bouncing it lightly against his hand to shake the lotion down.

Taylor gave him a withering look. "Thanks, but no thanks."

"You don't want to get burned the first day."

She pushed her dark glasses up on her nose, taking another look at him as she did. He looked like some island native, with his skin darkened to bronze, a string of shells tied around his neck. His sun-streaked hair hung nearly to his shoulders and clearly hadn't seen a comb in days, nor had the stubble that darkened his chin seen a razor. The only jarring note was struck by his eyes, that sea-green that glowed all the brighter against his tan. Eyes that watched her with the lively pleasure of a cat watching a mouse it was toying with.

His teeth gleamed in a smile. "I suppose you could move your lounger into the shade. I'll help you if you want to get up." He gave her a guileless look.

It sent her blood to simmer. "Mr. Carson," she began.

"Dev," he corrected her.

"Dev. I'm sure you have other things to do today." *Besides heckling me.*

"I'm on vacation," he said lightly. "I don't have any plans at all."

"Well good," she said thinly. "I'm sure that will be fun for you. And while you're doing that, I'm going into the water. Can you please hand me my top?"

she asked with the studied aplomb she used for problem clients.

"Sure."

This was it, Taylor told herself with a swallow. The moment of truth. Then she heard the Italian woman laugh and she raised her chin a fraction. She wasn't going to make a fool of herself by trying to wriggle into the top without showing anything. She wasn't going to hide out like some bashful girl. Dammit, they were just breasts, and he'd already gotten an eyeful. Taylor pushed herself abruptly into a sitting position.

But Dev had already turned away to watch the dive boat come in to the dock that snaked out from the beach. "Are you going diving while you're here?"

"No," Taylor said shortly, fumbling to untangle her bikini top and slide her arms through the shoulder straps.

"Those reefs are about the most beautiful things I've ever seen," he said reflectively. "Like underwater palaces."

"My idea of vacation is lying on the beach and doing absolutely nothing."

With impeccable timing that she suddenly knew was entirely calculated, Dev turned back to her just as she got her top in place. It was impossible not to like him for it.

"Have you been to this area before?" he asked.

"Nope, this is my first time."

"Then you've got to get out to see the reefs, at least once. Don't you want to be able to tell your clients about it?"

"I'll show them pictures." Taylor stood up. "You can keep your crack-of-dawn scuba trips. I'll settle for sleeping in."

"Let me know if I can help."

She almost gave a snort of laughter before she caught herself. "Thanks but no thanks. I'll see you around. I'm going into the water."

Dev rose and sat on the edge of a nearby lounger. "You go right ahead." He looked her up and down and his grin widened. "I'll just sit here and enjoy the view."

Taylor walked down to the water, excruciatingly aware of the swing of her arms, every sway of her hips. Excruciatingly aware of Dev's eyes on her. She was being silly, she chided herself. He'd harassed her, had his laugh. With all the bare breasts around, he had to have lost interest in her. Still, she could feel two spots burning on the scrap of fabric that stretched over her haunches. Just her imagination, she told herself firmly, she'd look back and he'd be gone. As she stepped onto the damp, firm-packed sand by the water, she glanced over her shoulder toward her palapa. And saw Dev raise a hand lazily, his white smile glittering even from this distance.

Taylor flushed and stepped into the wash of foam.

SHE HAD DIED AND GONE TO heaven. That was simply all there was to it. Tropical sea, an aqua so pale it was luminous, stretched around her. She sank down in the water and looked along the shore to where the pastel wavelets met the periwinkle sky. No wonder everyone dressed in such bright colors in the tropics, they were trying to keep up with the exuberant background.

The gentle nudge of the foot high swells cradled her body. Even though she'd gone past the end of the dive dock to the string of cork floaters that marked the edge of the swim area, she was only chest deep in the warm water, her feet still touching ground. Bright-colored fish whisked along, past the occasional trail of seaweed. The water was clear enough that she could see the shadow patterns of the surface ripples waving on the bottom, could see the vivid red of her toenail polish against the white sand.

Taylor turned lightly to look at the gleaming beach that ran along the coast to where it curved out of sight. The graceful curves of coconut palm fronds swayed over the golden sand, dotted among the thatched palapas.

It was paradise.

Almost paradise, she corrected herself. Except for Dev Carson. Maybe if she spent a dozen years around him, she might stop turning red every time she saw him. It probably wouldn't happen anytime soon, though.

She scowled at the tiny figures on the shore. Maybe he'd tired of teasing her by now and would leave her in peace. She thought of the spark of mischief in those green eyes and shook her head. She should be so lucky.

Diving under the water like a seal, she came up with her hair wet and slicked back. It was a shame. The more she thought about the idea of cutting loose for a totally meaningless and completely decadent vacation fling, the more it appealed to her. If Dev Carson had been just another guest at the resort, she'd have given very serious thought to jumping his bones. Granted, her bones-jumping skills were rusty, but there had been a time when she'd been able to reel in any man she set her cap for. She still had the equipment, she had no doubt she could do it again. She just needed to get back the mindset.

Somehow, though, none of the other men she'd seen around the resort had made quite the impression on her that Dev did. If only he weren't focused on their little contretemps.

Taylor rolled over to float lazily on her back, staring at the small white puffs of cloud in the sky overhead. She couldn't do anything more about the situation than she already had. Ignore him and relax, that was the thing to do. This was her long overdue vacation. No way was she going to waste another precious minute of it worrying about work-related stuff. For the next seven days, duty and responsibility didn't exist. Indulging herself was the only rule.

That, and finding herself a decadent summer lover.

DUSK WAS PURPLING TO evening as Taylor strolled up the winding jungle trail that led from her room to the restaurant. Stone lanterns dotting the side of the path cast a soft, peach glow over the flagstones, illuminating the nodding blossoms on plantings by the trail. Out in the dim space under the trees, a bird whistled softly. The skirt of her hot pink minidress swished against her thighs. With every step, she felt the years slough away, bringing her closer to the carefree, happy-go-lucky chance-taker she had once been.

She'd begun to relax fractionally that afternoon after she returned to her lounger to find Dev Carson nowhere in sight. The little prick of disappointment she'd felt, she'd suppressed ruthlessly. No mixing business and pleasure, she told herself sternly. Having a fling would be wonderful. Having a fling with Dev Carson would be the dumbest thing she could do.

But he was gone, and hopefully that was the end of it. She ignored the tiny voice in her head—miniscule, really—that whined about the rarity of six-pack abs. He was gone and she was glad. Now she could relax and take it easy. After all, in a resort of nearly a thousand people, she might go days without seeing him again.

But she'd kept her top on the rest of the afternoon, just in case.

The path leveled and broadened and changed into polished golden terrazzo that led along the edge of the open-air restaurant. In a region where the air was warm and silky, even in winter, walls were superfluous. The only thing necessary was the thatched roof that hung down at the edges and soared to a peak in the center, blocking out the occasional cloudbursts. Long ponds patrolled by orange and white koi separated the walkway from the dining area, where a fringe of dried palm fronds overhung the edge of the roof. One side of the restaurant looked out on a broad waterfall that cascaded over rocks, the chatter of the droplets soothing in her ears.

Taylor walked up to the hostess stand at the entrance. *"Hola, señorita,"* smiled a compact, dark-eyed man, with a badge that said Raoul. "You wish for dinner?" he asked.

"Si, gracias," Taylor replied. *"Un asiento, por favor."*

"Ah." His eyes lit. *"Habla Español?"*

Taylor laughed and held her forefinger and thumb half an inch apart. *"Un poquito, un poquito,"* she said, shaking her hand ruefully.

Raoul picked up a menu and led her to the side of the restaurant near the waterfall where a stream of droplets fell musically into the catch basin. The paddles of overhead fans stirred the air. Candles flickered on the tables and soft Latin guitar played over the sound system. It was exquisite. She wouldn't have changed a thing.

Except for the fact that the table Raoul was leading her toward was already occupied by Dev Carson.

He stood up as Raoul stopped at the table, and pulled out a chair for her. *"Gracias, amigo,"* he said, nodding to Raoul.

"De nada," Raoul murmured with a wink and disappeared.

Taylor looked at Dev and he looked steadily back. Behind him, the drops of the backlit waterfall chattered. His tan was dark against the white linen of his shirt. His eyes glimmered with something like anticipation, and had something in her stomach chittering like the waterfall.

"Hot-pink suits you."

Taylor took a deep breath and let it out slowly, letting her system steady. "Mr. Carson," she began.

"Dev," he corrected.

"So you keep telling me. Look, I know you weren't happy with the way things worked out at the travel agency, and I sympathize with that. I sympathize with the fact that you might still be annoyed. But I'm on vacation. You made your point this afternoon. I'd be happy to listen to anything else you have to say—next week, in my office. While I'm here, I'm off the clock. *Buenos noches.*" She moved to turn away.

He took a step and was at her side. "Don't go. Have dinner with me."

She blinked at him.

"Just dinner. I'm not going to give you a bad time. I swear," he said, holding up his hands, palms toward her. "Baltimore never happened. *Pffffttt.*" At her suspicious look, he went back to his seat. "Look, I've been down here for three weeks. I've gotten certified for scuba and dived half a dozen reefs, some of them twice. I've parasailed. I've been to see the ruins. I've taken a catamaran around the island. I've made friends with all the staff. It would be nice for a change to talk to someone who wasn't paid to be friendly to me."

A quick frisson of sympathy whisked through her. Taylor sat down slowly. "Somehow, I have a feeling that the only time you dine alone is when you want to."

"I haven't exactly been in the mood for company, at least I wasn't at first. I've been…mellowing over the past week," he decided.

Somehow, mellow wouldn't have been the word she would have chosen. True, he lounged in the chair across from her, but it was with the watchful indolence of some beast that could spring on its prey without warning. And she had the uneasy feeling that despite his assurances, his prey just might be her.

The waiter stopped by to take their drink orders. Dev eyed her as she asked for a beer. "You're in Mexico," he said. "Why not a shot of tequila?"

She looked at him for a moment. *Six-pack abs,* the voice whispered. "Why not? A shot please," she asked the waiter.

"Herradura, por favor," Dev added, *"y dos cervezas."*

"What's Herradura?" Taylor asked suspiciously as the waiter left.

"Top quality tequila, the kind that you don't need salt and a lime to get down. You can sip this stuff," he added, nodding at the bottle that the waiter was bringing their way.

"A connoisseur?" she asked, raising a brow.

He shrugged. "Three weeks in Mexico will teach you a thing or two if you're prepared to listen instead of talk."

Somehow she could see that about him, a certain quiet watchfulness that absorbed the world around him. The waiter set the shot glasses on the table and poured the amber liquid, then nodded and left.

Dev picked up his glass. "Here's to vacations."

"To vacations," she echoed and took a sip of the tequila. To her surprise, it flowed down smooth and warm, though with a fiendish little kick at the end. Savoring the flavor, she glanced up to see Dev watching her.

"Like it?"

She nodded, taking another sip. "I'm surprised. In college we always did the whole salt and lime routine. I thought you had to."

"Only with cheap rotgut tequila. The salt and lime is just to cover up the taste. The good stuff like this is made for sipping," he said, demonstrating.

"Mmm. Could be dangerous. A sip here, a sip there, and the next thing you know you're hammered and dancing on the tables."

His eyes lit with interest. "Now that I'd like to see."

"Don't hold your breath," she laughed.

"So what if you dance on the tables? Isn't that what vacations are for? No one knows you here."

"Except you."

"I'll never tell. This is time-out from the real world, you can do whatever you like. And, you know, if what you'd like is to dance on the tables, I'm all in support of that."

"You're so generous."

"Aren't I, though," he said modestly. "So if you're not going to dance on the tables, what are you going to do?"

She moved her glass meditatively in a little circle on the table. "I don't know, probably as little as possible. I haven't had a break in almost five years. I keep catching myself starting to think about work and I have to remind myself to let it go."

"It takes a couple of days, at least it did for me. Especially if you're down here with no distractions."

"When was the last time you had a vacation?"

"I'm not sure I've ever really had one," he said thoughtfully. "Not like this, anyway."

"Relaxation makes you live longer."

"So does being able to afford groceries." He shrugged. "I've mostly been running my own business for the past ten years. It takes over your life. I'm sure you can relate."

"What do you do?"

"Ah, ah, ah." He shook his finger at her. "Baltimore doesn't exist, remember? No talking about the real world and definitely no talking about work." His eyes lingered on her as the waiter set their beers on the table. Dev reached out to take his glass, held it up. "Here's to being off the clock."

The clink of glass rang in the warm evening air.

"So you said you're going to do as little as possible. What does that mean?"

She shrugged. "Lie on the beach, sleep in, read

books.'' She didn't figure adding wild sex to that list would be wise, although she was suddenly certain he'd be happy to volunteer. And as the tequila flowed through her veins, she was beginning to think it wouldn't be such a bad idea. In fact, if his current mood held, Dev Carson might be just what the doctor ordered. ''I figure I'll just relax for a week. Maybe dance a little, flirt a little. I'm on vacation, after all.''

''So you are. Well, it is an all-inclusive resort. I think flirtations are part of the list of services. Did I mention,'' he asked casually, ''that Raoul considers me an honorary local?''

She looked at him consideringly. ''Can I take that to mean you're offering to be of service?''

He sat up and leaned forward. ''Oh, service is the name of my game, Ms. DeWitt. Satisfaction guaranteed.''

It was ridiculous to start a flirtation with someone from home, she thought. *Baltimore doesn't exist,* the words played through her head. *Isn't that what vacations are for?* Maybe. And maybe it was time to let the old Taylor come out to play.

HE'D NEVER SEEN A WOMAN GO into ecstasy over mango cheesecake before, Dev reflected as he watched Taylor eat her dessert. Her tongue flicked out to catch a crumb of crust, and his pulse bumped for a moment.

It had been doing that a lot in the past couple of hours.

Dev Carson considered himself smart, tough, ambitious and focused. When he decided to go after something—or someone—he was usually successful. What he wanted, he got.

And he wanted Taylor DeWitt in the worst way. At first, it had been a game: embarrass her a little, have some fun flirting. Somehow over the course of the day and evening, she'd become an unendurable temptation, a prospect of pleasure that drummed through his mind.

Watching her eat had been a revelation. Unlike most women, she didn't pick at her food but dug in with enthusiasm and little hums of satisfaction. She sampled every exotic dish offered at the show-cooking buffet, experiencing it with an exquisite pleasure that had him imagining what she would look like in the throes of orgasm. After he'd taken her there.

Taylor pushed her plate away. "That was fabulous."

"You looked like you were enjoying it."

"Especially since someone else is doing the cooking and cleaning. But I'm stuffed. If I don't move soon, you're going to have to carry me to my room."

Now that was a prospect with some possibilities, he thought. "Just say the word."

Taylor laughed. "I think I can walk for now, I just need to be encouraged a bit."

Dev rose and held out his hand. "I can help with that."

The sultry strains of Latin music floated into the night sky as they approached the open-air theater area. Soft light filtered down onto the dance floor, where couples swayed to the slow, hypnotic beat from the band.

Dev took her hand. "Dance with me?"

Taylor lifted a brow. "Fred, I thought you'd never ask."

"You laugh, but prepare to be amazed and humbled."

"Another one of the things you've picked up since you've been here?"

"I like to consider myself a multifaceted individual."

He led her down the steps and onto the polished wood floor. Taylor looked at the couples nestled together. Anticipation sent a sharp thrill through her, then he swept her in toward him, unexpectedly close.

She'd expected the classic clinch and shuffle of the high school slow dance, but he surprised her, capturing one of her hands in his and pressing his other against the small of her back. The heat spread through the thin silk of her dress, making her catch her breath.

Making her melt against him.

"I don't know how to dance like this," she said unsteadily, clutching at his shoulder with her free hand. His hard, rounded shoulder. "I only ever learned to shuffle around."

"It's a rumba," he murmured in her ear, "a standard box step. Just hold on and follow me."

The guitar moaned low and soft over the clicking tropical rhythm of a hollow woodblock. An exotic woman dressed in fiery red stepped up to the microphone and began to croon in Spanish, a passionate tale of what Taylor figured was no doubt doomed lovers.

Moving in time with Dev's body was immensely seductive. She felt the muscles of his thighs flex against hers. She looked up and found her gaze snared by his, the green shadowed in the dim lighting. He brought their clasped hands in close to their bodies, pressing her against him. The call of the guitar drifted up into the sky.

THEY STROLLED DOWN the shadowed path that wound through the jungle toward the beach. Dev tangled his fingers with Taylor's. "I couldn't believe it when I first got down here," he murmured. "I thought I'd walked into another world. Home was gone." It hadn't been quite as easy as that, if he was honest. It had taken days in the hot sun, hours of swimming with the schools of bright fish in the tranquil blue depths of the reefs to erase the memory of finding his fiancée with another man. No matter that he'd known deep down they were a bad match, the betrayal had scored his pride. To smooth it over, he'd flirted with a couple of the beach babes but something had felt wrong each time. Each time, he'd ducked out with a simple kiss good-night.

Somehow, he didn't see himself doing that with Taylor.

They followed the trail out of the lush plantings to circle around the edge of the pool, now glowing pale turquoise. At this hour, the area was deserted, the guests all up at the theater area dancing and watching the show. They had the beach to themselves.

A vivid red hibiscus blossom, fallen from its bush, lay on the pavement. Dev stopped to pick it up. Turning to Taylor, he tucked it behind her ear. "Now you look like an island girl."

"You're the one who looks like an islander, with that tan and the batik and the shells…"

He fingered them. "The clerk at the hotel store threw them in when I bought my trunks."

"I don't have to ask if she was a she," Taylor said dryly.

"She was indeed, and also about sixteen. Not my style."

"You're not into giggling Mark Anthony fans?"

"I'm not into girls." His eyes darkened. "I'm more interested in women."

Taylor swallowed and the silence stretched out for a beat, then two. In the darkness, the crude stone heads of the showers had a brooding, almost menacing cast, like vengeful gods come down to earth. Beyond, Dev could hear the hiss of the waves. He reached out and caught her hand again. "Let's go out by the water."

The moonlit beach was dotted with the shadowed bulk of palms. They slipped off their shoes and stepped onto the sand. Away from people and noise, Taylor could hear the small rustles of the night creatures going about their business. To one side, a crab scuttled into a stand of mangrove. And the waves grew louder.

Dev led her past the palm trees and onto the dock. Their feet made hollow thumps as they walked along the creosote coated planks. Thick ropes swung from squat posts, making only a passing pretense at security. It didn't matter, really; in such shallow, warm water, a person falling in could hardly get hurt. Out on the end of the dock, a red light atop a tall post winked out to sea.

The water stretched away from them black and fathomless. Far in the distance, on the coast of the mainland, a few lights glimmered. Above them, stars painted their patterns on a midnight velvet sky.

Dev looked up at them. "The stars are different

down here, have you noticed?'' Somehow, that had been the thing that had finally allowed him to let go the frustration and betrayal, that sense of being somewhere different. He'd come out to the dock at night a lot those first weeks. Gradually, the peace had seeped into his soul. ''That was the first thing I looked for down here, the Southern Cross.'' He pointed. ''You can barely see it on the horizon.''

Taylor stepped close to him and he felt the soft swell of her breasts brush against his arm. ''Where?''

He moved so that she was in front of him and pointed over one of her shoulders so she could sight along his finger. ''There, there, and…there.''

''Do you know any other constellations?''

''I was pretty into it when I was a kid.'' It had been a good excuse to get out of the house and away from the fighting. ''There's Sagittarius and Scorpio,'' he said, pointing them out. Taylor's hair brushed against his arm, silky and light.

''How come all of the constellations are always critters?''

''They're not. You've got Perseus and Orion, they were warriors, and Cassiopiea, she was a seer.''

''Always alone, though. Don't you think all those lonely shepherds that named the original constellations would have seen lovers somewhere?''

''Sure. They just didn't make it into the astronomy books.''

She leaned back against him and he wrapped his arms around her. ''I like the idea of lovers painted on the sky.''

''How about earthbound lovers?'' He nuzzled her hair, breathing in her scent.

Taylor turned in his arms. In her eyes, he read

promise, challenge and mischief. Then she pressed her mouth to his. It jolted through him down to his toes. He made himself concentrate on the soft, nibbling temptation, holding back from letting his hands rove over her body, that sleek, alluring frame. He could taste the faint sweetness of the margarita she'd had at the theater.

Then she stepped away. "How about lovers in the water?" she asked, dropping her shoes.

Exhilaration tore through him. "You don't have a suit," he pointed out.

"Mmm, you're right, and I'd hate to ruin this nice dress." She reached down and pulled the pink silk up, sliding it off over her head.

Underneath, she wore nothing.

His mouth went dry. Her skin glowed pale and lovely in the moonlight, rounded breasts tipped with the darker shadows of her aureole. Before he could look his fill, she turned and walked to the edge of the dock.

"I think you're running behind, Mr. Carson. You'd better catch up," she said, flashing a look at him over her shoulder.

And dove into the water.

3

THE SALTWATER CLOSED AROUND her body and slid against her skin, warm as an embrace. Like a sea creature, she arrowed through the water, feeling a rush of illicit arousal at the brush of liquid against her bare nipples, her bare behind. She burst up through the surface laughing at her own audacity.

And blinked. The dock was empty in the moonlight. Taylor gave a quick glance around, raking her fingers through her wet hair. He was here somewhere, she knew. A man like Dev Carson didn't walk away from a challenge. She felt the thrill of expectation.

Then the water next to her exploded and she jumped and whirled to see him rearing out of the water.

She put a hand to her chest, suddenly intensely aware of her bare breasts above the waterline. "You just took ten years off my life, you know."

"Did you think I was a sea monster?"

Actually, with the water streaming from his shoulders and his hair soaked and disheveled, she thought he looked more like some kind of a sea god. A surge of anticipation ran through her as he moved nearer. "You can never tell what's swimming around," she said, then blinked as he disappeared. Seconds ticked by, then she jumped at the feeling of a slippery hand sliding down her back.

He surfaced a few feet away. "Well, you know, you're taking your chances, swimming at night. You never know what's going to decide to take a bite out of you." He stepped closer and a little shiver of anticipation ran through her.

"I know. Something just fondled me," she said.

"Those damned fish are getting more forward all the time."

"Maybe it wasn't a fish. Maybe it was some other kind of critter."

"All the more reason you should stay close so I can protect you. I'll keep an eye out for the bad guys."

"You must have good night vision." She swayed lightly in the soft pressure of a swell.

"I eat lots of carrots."

"Planning ahead?"

"It never hurts to be prepared."

"Were you a Boy Scout?"

He laughed, a low, rough sound in the dark. "No, I hung with a more disreputable crowd."

It had her pulse thumping. "Maybe I should go in, then. A young lady's known by the company she keeps."

His teeth gleamed in the dim lighting. "Did you learn that from your mama?"

"From cotillion, thank you very much."

"Somehow you don't seem like the type to get too caught up in rules. After all, the signs say no skinny dipping."

"I wanted to go swimming," she said with dignity.

"Without a suit?"

"I'm impatient." Somehow, she was breathless, even though she hadn't moved.

"So am I." His eyes were shadowed. The moonlight had leached the color out so that they just seemed to glow silver.

"What are you impatient for?"

He skimmed a hand across the water between them and stepped a bit closer. "You."

Taylor stared at him, watched him come near. Then she whipped out of the way, swimming past him so that she brushed his legs. His fingers started to close around her ankle, but she whisked past. When she felt him stroking after her, she abruptly reversed direction in a flip turn and surfaced, breathing hard.

Dev came out of the water a few feet away from her. "Playing cat and mouse?"

"Or shark and angelfish."

"Are you calling me an angel?" His eyes laughed at her, then he shook his head so that drops of water scattered around them.

"Somehow, you remind me more of a devil." This time when she ducked under the water, she brushed a hand down his ass, just to feel if it was as marble hard as the rest of him before she flicked away. Lightning fast, he turned and managed to stroke her leg as she flowed past and up to the surface.

"Careful when you go grabbing like that, darlin'," he said when he'd followed her. "You might get hold of something I'll need later."

She laughed. "I don't know, if I were you, I'd worry more about some hungry little fishy thinking it's a big fat ol' worm dangling there and taking himself a nibble."

His teeth gleamed white in a smile that suddenly reminded her of the shark she'd mentioned. "It's not dangling like a worm right now."

Taylor ducked back under the water, this time
stroking a hand over his belly—oh, those rock-hard
abs—as she passed. She was just one beat too slow,
though. His hand slid down the length of her back,
curving over the taut muscle of her ass. Swiftly it
tightened around her ankle, pulling her back toward
him.

When his hand slid up over her bare breast, Taylor
jolted and reared her head up out of the water, gasping. It felt outrageous. It felt provocative.

It felt right.

Suddenly the mood of play was gone. She let her
feet touch the bottom, swaying lightly in the water.
Given that it had been years since she'd had sex with
anyone but herself in the room, the idea of a man
touching her was exciting and more than a little
frightening.

The reality of it was simply exciting, period.

Dev's face tightened and he stepped forward, pulling her against him.

Heat on heat, mouth on mouth, the stroke of hands
sending sensation rocketing through her body. Taylor
shuddered. God, it had been so long since it had been
like this, maybe even never. Surely she'd have remembered this kind of kaleidoscopic physical rush
sweeping her along into madness, she thought as Dev
crushed her mouth under his. Rough stubble scraped
against her skin. Tantalizing, it failed to satisfy but
only made her want more.

She clutched at his shoulders. Buoyed by the water,
she wrapped her legs around his waist. The smooth,
hard heat of his belly tormented her. She wanted him
in her, hard and against her. This had nothing to do

with tequila or vacation, it had to do with a wanting
that went deep into her bones.

Waves slapped softly at the pilings of the dive
dock. The palapa fronds rustled in the wind. The
brush of hand on skin was slick and silent, the shudders silent and swift.

Dev groaned at the feel of Taylor's breasts filling
his hands, her sleek, soft legs holding him in a slippery grip. He was so hard that he was brushing up
against the cleft between her buttocks, the slick touch
keeping him on the edge of coming. Not yet, though,
he thought. There were places he wanted to take her,
things he wanted her to feel before that.

He slid his hands around her back and pulled her
toward him, running his tongue tip along the impos-
sibly soft skin of her jawline, down her throat. He'd
wondered how she'd tasted. He'd thought about it all
day, as they'd sat at dinner, as they'd walked down
the beach in the darkness. The combination of smooth
softness and sleek strength enthralled him. To have
her now, filling his arms, pressed up against him,
robbed him of breath, rendered him rock hard with
need. He wanted to make her blind with pleasure,
immersed in heat, to send her flying over the edge.

"Tell me you want this," he muttered, running a
hand down the flat of her belly.

Taylor gasped and arched against him. "I want
you," she whispered.

He filled his hands with her breasts again, feeling
the soft give and the hard tips against his palms. Unable to hold back, he lowered his head to take her
nipple into his mouth. The feel of the rough nub
against his tongue sent sudden, sharp arousal jolting
through him. His fingers slid lower, passing curls of
hair to find her wet in a way that had nothing to do

with water. Knowing she was right there, accessible, threatened his control, but didn't break it. Though he ached to drive his cock into her, he held back. Instead he found the hard, tight bud of her clit.

Taylor jolted in shock at the hands of another on that most sensitive of spots. The slight calluses on the ends of his fingers teased a thousand nerve endings with slippery friction. She strained against him with a moan, as the tension coiled in her. His fingers tormented, then teased, then stroked rhythmically, leaving her helpless to do anything but feel.

Pumping her hips to accentuate his touch, she moved against the maddening strokes. His hand tightened on her breast, squeezing the nipple and she climaxed in a rush of sensation that exploded through every cell, crying out and gasping with the intensity, her body bucking helplessly against him.

Taylor clung to him as the shudders ebbed slowly away. Then her eyes met his, and the desire flared up again, hot and immediate. She pulled his head down to hers for a fierce, fast kiss, running her hands down the taut, corrugated muscles of his belly, feeling them raise up against her fingertips. "I think we need to do something to equalize things." She slid off of him to stand on legs that were still trembling. Reaching out, she wrapped her fingers around his erection, but he stilled her hand.

"I've got a better idea. Let's go back to my room."

She nipped his lips. "For a bed?"

He wrapped his hand around her neck and pulled her close for a hard kiss. "For a condom."

THE DOOR SLAMMED BEHIND THEM and Dev pressed Taylor against the wall, feeling the soft spring of her muscles against him.

"You're wearing too many clothes," he muttered distractedly. "I want you naked and I want to be in you."

"Mmm." She kissed him, and reached down for the hem of her dress. "Then maybe we'd better stop wasting time." She pulled it over her head and dropped it in a pool of pink silk on the tile floor.

Dev slid his hands down the smooth curves of her waist, brushing over her backside for a heady instant before he moved his hands up into her hair and kissed her hard, feeling the soft strands spilling over his fingers. Then he pressed her back to the wall, holding her in place as he knelt down and tormented her with his mouth and tongue.

She writhed against him until he could feel how wet she was, taste how close she was to the edge. And he stopped, wanting, needing to see her face this time in the light, to watch her flush as her orgasm moved through her.

When he stood, it was her hands that tugged feverishly at the drawstring on his pants. When he pushed the cloth down, it was her hands that searched him out where he was heavy and hard, jerking just a little with the force of his arousal. And when he stepped forward, it was her hands that guided him inside, her moans that filled the room when his own voice failed and all he could do was gasp at the tight, hot miracle of her body clenched around him.

RED-GOLD LIGHT STAINED Dev's eyelids. He moved to roll away from it, to burrow back down into sleep, but he couldn't move. His arm was numb, held down by a solid weight.

A weight of warm, soft female flesh.

He gathered the bundle against him even as he rose into consciousness, a consciousness laced with sensory snapshots—the maddening moments before they'd reached his room…the yielding heat of her naked body against his…the hot, slick rush as he slid himself into her…the molten explosion of his orgasm into her still shuddering body. And all the times they repeated it in the hours that followed.

Dev pressed a kiss on the tousle of blond hair and Taylor grumbled once in slumber.

"Shhh," he whispered. "You can go back to sleep, just let me get my arm out." It felt more like a chunk of wood than an arm, but he moved it nonetheless. Enduring its wake-up promised to be excruciating.

Taylor rolled away from him and burrowed back into the pillow, the sheet falling away from her to reveal an enticingly angular back. Dev looked at it speculatively, but then tingling in his fingertips warned him that the fun was just beginning. Minutes ticked by while he suffered through pins and needles, focusing on the curves of her body in an effort to distract himself.

He shifted onto his side to stare at Taylor in the dim light of the room and stroked a hand down her back, savoring the way it sloped down and then rose in a tight curve.

She rolled onto her stomach and turned her face to him, squinting at him through her mop of hair. "It can't possibly be morning. What time is it?"

"You're in Neverland, darlin', there are no clocks. Close your eyes and go back to sleep."

Tempting though the prospect was, it wasn't nearly that easy. She was in the bed of a person she hardly knew after a one-night stand. A memorable one-night stand, but a one-night stand nevertheless. It had been a long time, but as she recalled, the drill was to wake up and leave as soon as possible. Groaning, she pushed herself up to sit on the edge of the bed, feeling the unaccustomed soreness between her thighs. They'd used each other hard and relentlessly, she remembered, stretching in a pleasurable satisfaction.

She yawned. "Give me just a minute and I'll get out of your hair." The next second she was squawking as Dev pulled her back to tumble against him in a welter of sheets and pillows.

"Who said I wanted you to?" He scooped her in to spoon against him, his chest warm against her back, his thighs strong and solid underneath hers.

"Well, I just figured this was..." Her voice trailed off as she felt his tongue trace the line of her shoulder.

"This was what?" Dev murmured in her ear. His hand slid over to one of her breasts, brushing the fragile skin and squeezing the nipple.

"A one-night stand," she managed. "A fling."

He bit her earlobe lightly. "A fling, certainly. But I never recall any discussion of a time limit." His other hand slid down between her thighs to find where she was already slippery. "We've got the whole rest of the week. I was hoping to talk you into something a little more leisurely. I've definitely got no interest in letting you walk away this morning."

She could feel him hardening against her bottom. "I just don't..." His fingers moved against her, forcing a moan from her.

"You don't think you could walk out of here this morning without coming at least once? Smart girl," he said approvingly.

Clever and slick, his fingers slid against her clit.
The bolts of sensation had her moving her hips helplessly. Reaching back, Taylor pulled his face toward
hers. His mouth. She wanted his mouth, then his cock,
as deep as he could go. "I need you in me," she
whispered against his lips.

"Always happy to oblige a lady," he returned,
shifting so that she was beneath him.

"CAN YOU JUST CARRY ME to the beach?" Dev
groaned.

"You were the one who had the big idea about
round two," Taylor said, rolling over to prop her arms
on his chest.

"I've always been the kind of guy who sticks with
what works."

Taylor fought to keep a straight face. "And in this
case?"

"Well, round one worked, and round two worked.
I think we ought to stretch it out a little more." He
stroked her back and she purred like a cat.

"What did you have in mind?" she asked, pressing
little kisses on his jaw.

"We're both here the rest of the week." He held
up her left hand and inspected it. "No tan lines. Good.
You appear to be footloose and fancy free and God
knows I am. I got blood tests for the wedding, so I'm
healthy and clean. How about you?"

"I give blood monthly."

"So we're set there. What do you say?"

"About?"

"About making a week of it."

"Sleeping together, you mean?"

He nodded. "Unless you were faking it and really

didn't have a good time. It's perfect. No ties, no commitments, just whatever we want, whenever we want.''

"And nothing when we get home.'' She didn't phrase it as a question.

He shook his head. "Nothing when we get home. You can do anything and everything your heart desires and know you'll never have to face me again.''

"If you agree to it, you've got to mean it," Taylor warned. "No looking me up after we get home.''

He leaned in and bit her shoulder. "Not that you aren't completely delectable, but after what I went through a couple of weeks ago, darlin', I'm not exactly leaping out of my skin to get involved in another relationship.''

Taylor looked at him consideringly. "How's your stamina? I've gone without for quite a while. Whenever I want might be pretty often. I'd hate to choose you over some of the other guys around here and find out that I've worn you out.''

He silenced her with his mouth. "Well, you can stop your search right here. I'm all the man you're going to need.''

"Oh, yeah?''

He curved his hand over her breast. "I'm up to the task.''

"Oh, yeah?'' she asked, her hand straying down to find that he was, indeed, up. "Oh,'' she said softly, "yeah.''

"I take my vitamins,'' he murmured.

"Good thing,'' she whispered against his mouth. "You're going to need them.''

4

———

"I LIKE YOUR ROOM BETTER than mine," Dev said, lying back watching Taylor change out of her clothes from the night before. The ceiling fan turned slowly, the woven bamboo paddles lazily stirring the air.

"It's no different than yours."

"Oh, yes, it is. You're standing in it. That makes all the difference." He rolled up onto one elbow and watched with interest as she worked her way into her bikini. "Let me know if you want some help with that," he added.

She shot him a look. "Oh, no, we're not going down that path again. I came down here to lie on the beach, not to stay in a room all day."

Dev rolled off the bed and onto his feet. "I don't know, it's a nice room," he said, looking around at the golden stucco walls dotted with mock Mayan artifacts. The coverlet and the couch held the vivid primary colors of a serape; the terrazzo floor was cool under his feet. "Besides, I can make it worth your while." He stepped up behind her and began unhooking her bikini top.

"Stop that," she laughed, swatting at him.

"What's this?" he asked, picking up a disposable camera sitting on the counter.

"What does it look like?" Taylor gave him an amused glance, then slipped on a tank top.

"You've only been here a day and you've already filled up a 36 exposure roll?"

She zipped up her shorts. "I've been taking photos of the resorts. I put them in a book back at the agency to show to customers when they ask."

"You've got one more shot on here, you know."

"Yeah." She headed to the bathroom to get more sunblock. "Toss it into my beach bag," she called. "I'll finish it up when we get down to the beach."

He watched her come back out into the room, slim and luscious, already with a faint golden glow to her skin. Desire tugged at him but he pushed it down. He wanted to see her out among other people. He wanted to see her smile at another and be able to look at her and know that she was his for the taking.

They left the room, threading their way along the winding walkway out to the lush jungle path that headed toward the beach. Dev caught at Taylor's elbow to stop her. "Up ahead," he said softly. Near the flagstone path stood a trio of exotic black birds with rolls of glossy black feathers that furled back from the tops of their heads. "They look like they got into a packet of Jheri Curl."

"Do you think we scared them?" she whispered, admiring their long sweeps of ebony tail feathers.

"Who knows? Maybe they get paid to stand around and look intriguing for the guests."

As though they'd heard his remark, the birds looked at them disdainfully, then turned and began stalking away deeper into the jungle.

"So much for the wildlife," she said.

Dev caught her around the waist. "I'll show you some wildlife."

"I bet you will, you—"

"Hola, amigos," said a voice behind them. Taylor turned to see Dev's crony from the restaurant the night before walking down the trail toward them. He was dressed this time in the royal-blue polo shirt and shorts of the Nova Friends, the resort's entertainment and recreation crew.

"Hola, Raoul," Dev said. "I don't think you two met properly last night. This is Taylor. Taylor, this is Raoul. He's a Nova Friend."

"But I thought you were working in the restaurant last night," she said in puzzlement.

He nodded. "Sometimes, when I am doing a favor, I will do that."

She looked at them suspiciously, wondering exactly who he'd been doing the favor for.

As though reading her mind, Dev smiled easily. "Raoul and I have done a little fishing and sailing while I've been here."

"Si, we are *amigos.* But you, *señorita,* are much prettier company than I am. I am afraid I will not see so much of Señor Dev before he leaves."

"Don't talk about leaving yet," Taylor protested. "I just got here. I don't ever want to go."

"But once you spend time in Mexico, you carry always a little piece of him with you. You can look at the pictures and return."

"Speaking of which, here's that camera," Dev said, pulling it out of his pocket and handing it to her. "Don't forget to finish it off."

"Ah, a camera." Raoul's eyes lit up and he reached out his hand. "If you will allow me, I will take a photo of you."

"Well, I don't think…" Taylor began.

Raoul took the camera neatly from her hands and

stepped back. "Ah, now, in such a romantic place, my friends, you must be romantic also."

She felt Dev's arms go around her from behind. "We don't need this," she said.

"Ah, you must be romantic," Dev murmured. "Say 'wild sex,'" he added, making her giggle just as Raoul snapped the shutter.

"It will be a beautiful picture," Raoul said, handing Dev the camera. "Do you go now to the beach? That is where I go, too. I will be starting a game of horseshoes, if you wish to join."

"It sounds fun, but I have a date with a book and a sun couch," Taylor said.

"Ah, you break my heart, *señorita*. Perhaps I will see you tonight at the show, though. We are having a dating game show. You could enter, maybe, if you are not already preoccupied." He grinned, his teeth very white against his skin. "Enjoy your day."

TAYLOR LAY ON HER LOUNGER, reading a novel.

"Hey baby," said a lounge lizard voice, "can I buy you a drink?"

She glanced up to see Dev standing by the sun couch, holding two plastic glasses. He leaned down to give her a quick, hard kiss that stretched into long minutes. Then an icy drop of condensation from one of the glasses dripped onto her bare breast and she gasped and jumped.

"Chilly?" he asked, reaching out with a fingertip to wipe the cool water away from where it trembled on her skin, just above her aureole.

She caught a breath at the brush of his finger. That was all it took, she marveled. Even after making love all night and all morning, it took just the merest touch to send her pulse thumping. She made a stab at a reproving look and reached for her glass. "No groping me on the beach, you."

"I bring you offerings of boat drinks and you scold me?" Dev stretched out on the lounger next to her and gave her a long, leisurely look. "I thought the rule was no rules."

"Not for us, but there might be Iberonova rules," she said, nodding toward the guard standing twenty yards away in his blue trousers and white tunic.

"You're cute." He leaned over to kiss her shoulder. "Trust me, Jorge is more interested in looking good for Marisa than in harassing an innocent guest brushing water off his lover."

She glanced over to where the guard brushed at his gold braid and preened for the barmaid. "You may have a point. In that case..." She moved her glass and let a bit more water drip on her breasts and shrugged enough to send a drop rolling toward her nipple.

"Now you're being cruel," he said, running the tip of his tongue across his lips.

"What do you mean?" she asked innocently, brushing the water away, watching his eyes darken.

"You're so bad," he said, shaking his head.

She took a sip of her margarita and settled back. "I'm just sitting here reading my book."

"Whatcha reading?"

"Find out for yourself," she suggested, handing over her book of erotic short stories. She watched as he read, his brows rising. After a few minutes, he handed it back to her and gave her a speculative glance. "Your mama know you read stuff like this?"

Taylor pushed her sunglasses down her nose and

gave him a wink. "I read at least two books off the *New York Times* notable books list each year. I chat with my mother about those and she's satisfied I'm looking after my intellect. The rest of the time I read to please me."

"Makes my Robert Parker look a whole lot less interesting." He paged back a little more. "No wonder you just wanted to lie on the beach and read."

"I always have my reasons for everything," she purred.

"So I see. Don't suppose I could get you to read me a bedtime story one of these nights, could I?"

"Only if you're really good."

"That sounds like a challenge to me," he said, stroking a hand up her leg.

A horn sounded as the dive boat came in to dock. With a hollow clanging, a pair of assistants from the dive shop trundled a small cart full of air tanks out to meet it. A straggling line of guests in wet suits, clutching masks and regulators followed.

Dev stared at the boat speculatively as it settled in at the dock to exchange old passengers for new, then turned to Taylor. "You sure I can't lure you out for a snorkeling trip?"

She adjusted her sunglasses. "Tanks and wet suits make me claustrophobic."

He reached out to encircle her ankle with his thumb and forefinger. "You don't need that for snorkeling. All you need is fins and a mask. And a bikini top, of course."

"I just want to lie here and relax."

"Look, it's only a half-day trip. You'll love it, I promise you."

"I don't know about this." She pushed her sunglasses down her nose to look at him, laughter in her eyes. "What if I do it and I don't like it? What do I get?"

Dev stroked her calf. "The trip will be my treat."

"Not good enough. You're asking me to give up a half day out of my vacation."

He nodded to her book. "I'll read you page 132, in glorious Sensaround."

"Promise?"

"Sure, if the *Iberonova* has a trapeze."

THE DIVE BOAT BOBBED in the blue water off the coast of the island, near the Columbia Shallows. It didn't bother Taylor to be in open water. The waves were gentle, and she was an experienced swimmer. She swished her fins experimentally and was gratified when she shot forward. She slid the mask down over her eyes.

"Okay, are you ready?" Dev asked from where he treaded water next to her.

"You guaranteed me this wasn't work," she reminded him, adjusting her mask.

"It hardly is when you've got fins on. Anyway, there's enough of a current that you only have to float and let the water take you. I can get you a life ring if you want," he said, with an impudent look.

"I can swim for myself, thanks."

"And look mighty good doing it," he added, ducking his head under the water to survey her. "I don't think I've seen this bikini before. I definitely haven't taken it off you."

"Well don't get any big ideas out here. We might lose it and some barracuda would be flouncing around in my suit."

"It probably wouldn't look nearly as sexy as you do," he offered, but she swatted his hand away.

"We're out here to see the reefs, remember? Now where are they?"

"Just look down."

Taylor blinked in surprise, then put her head down into the water. If she hadn't had a snorkel in her mouth, she'd have gasped. Below her spread a fairy land of unimaginable variety. Red-orange coral towers rose next to whitish tubes with pink centers. Fronds of kelp waved gracefully in the ocean currents. Sea sponges fanned out next to the solid, crenelated spheres of brain coral.

She ducked under the water and swam closer. A small school of mottled peach parrot fish wove along the edge of the reef, skimming over an octopus swirling gracefully along to its lair. Behind all of it was the intense, immense blue of the sea.

Taylor ran out of air and rose to the surface, blowing the water out of her snorkel as she did. She yanked her mask down to her neck and whooped.

Dev surfaced next to her. "What do you think?"

"It's amazing. I've never seen anything like it."

"Put your mask back on. You're just getting started."

Below her, the reef rose in a solid mass, separated in places into serene white towers. A school of tiny silver fish made its way along the edge of a reef and then with no apparent provocation made an abrupt shift to the right before swimming forward again.

Time stretched out, paced by the measured sound of her breath in the snorkel, by the infinite peace that stretched below her. In the cool blue twilight of the sea was a world of color and mystery.

Dev swam up to her, pointing downward and then to his chest. Understanding, she took a trio of deep breaths to charge her lungs and then they were swimming down, hand in hand. A puffer fish floated by, looking like a large, spiny sphere. She felt her ears pop as the reef rose alongside her, and she felt more a part of the ocean than ever. Dev gestured toward the reef, and she saw it. At a dark hollow in the coral, the glittering eyes of a moray eel stared back at her. She looked up, and somehow it was the surface and the air above that looked like another world, and the sea around her that seemed like home.

Then her lungs began to burn and she swam for the surface. She broke through to the air, trying to absorb the wonder. Dev rose next to her. "There's so much to see, I can't stay down there long enough," she said shaking her head.

"We've got more time. Take a deep breath and we'll go back down." His mouth curved. "Unless it's too much work for you."

She splashed him and dove under.

THE ENGINE OF THE BOAT vibrated and rumbled, taking them back to the resort. Taylor sat on the padded boat seat. "That coral that was like fairy fans, it was so gorgeous. And did you see the school of those fish with the yellow edging?" She was too wired to relax as she pulled on her tank top.

"Angelfish," he said, watching in bemusement at her bright-eyed pleasure. He hadn't quite understood the impulse that had led him to cajole and persuade until he'd talked her into going out to the reefs. He'd only known he'd wanted her to experience it. The underwater universe had been a revelation to him.

When he found that she'd never been, he'd suddenly found himself consumed with helping her discover it. "Now you see why I wanted to bring you out here?"

"It's wonderful." She leaned in to kiss him, lingering with her forehead pressed to his. "Thank you for giving this to me. Now take me for a real dive."

"Really?"

She nodded. "I want to go deeper and stay down longer. Will you teach me?"

"We can get you qualified tomorrow and be diving by afternoon. Just say the word."

"Yes."

"Yes to what?"

She threw her arms around his neck and gave him a smacking kiss. "Yes to everything."

The dive captain passed around a cutting board with spears of pineapple on it. Taylor picked up one of the juicy spears and took a bite.

Dev leaned back against the cushions, watching her suck the spear of pineapple. She took another bite, then held it out to him. "Have some. It's good for what ails you."

He leaned closer to her. "You're good for what ails me," he said softly, pressing a kiss on her lips. Then he took a bite from the spear. The tart, sweet flavor banished the saltwater taste from his mouth, just as her simple joy banished the memory of his self-absorbed ex. "Now I seem to remember that we'd arranged a guarantee in the event you didn't like the trip, but we never discussed any kind of tip or compensation for me if I turned you on to something good."

"I didn't realize you were doing this for a fee," she said in amusement, popping the final bite of pineapple into her mouth, then holding her hand over the side to rinse it in the spray from the boat.

He clicked his tongue at her. "You of all people should realize that no service comes free."

"And here I thought this was an all-inclusive resort. What do you expect for payment?"

He tipped his head to one side, considering. Then a slow grin spread across his face. "Surprise me."

BY THE TIME THE BOAT DOCKED, the gathering clouds had coalesced into a tropical downpour. They hadn't even reached the end of the dive dock before they were soaked.

"So much for the beach," Taylor said as they stood under the eaves at the dive shop. "What do you want to do?"

Dev looked at the water streaming down from the palm thatching of the eaves. "Everybody at the resort is probably over at the big lunch palapa. Are you hungry?"

"Not very."

"I say we just go back to one of the rooms. Of course, we'll have to think of a way to keep ourselves busy." He cocked his head and looked at her.

Taylor stepped up and pressed him against the stucco wall of the dive shop. "I'm sure we'll come up with something," she whispered, her lips just a hairsbreadth from his. Then she turned and walked away without a backward glance.

She'd only gone about three steps when Dev's arm looped around her from behind and he pulled her around to face him. Then his mouth was on hers, his hands were fusing the two of them together and he was kissing her mindless while the warm rain sluiced

down over them. Their saturated clothing might as
well not have been there for all the good it did. Maybe
she wasn't naked, but with his hands on her, she felt
as though she were. Lightning crackled nearby, flashing blue light through her closed eyelids.

Dev broke away. "Let's get under cover before we
wind up getting barbecued."

"Good idea."

They went to her room because it was closer. Inside, the room was dark and cool. Taylor went over
to open the drapes, skidding a bit on the smooth tile,
and stepped outside to enjoy the fury of the storm.
Something about the tropical cloudbursts of Cozumel
made the hairs on the back of her neck stand up.
Perhaps it was their suddenness—one minute everything was sunny and warm, the next her senses were
overwhelmed with torrential rain, with bolts of lightning tinted pale pink or yellow or blue. Perhaps it
spoke to some primitive part of her that she'd inherited from her caveman forebears, when lightning
storms meant danger.

Rain came down in a loud rush, dripping from the
thatched roof that overhung her third floor balcony.
She loved the view from this room, treetop level, high
enough to be away from prying eyes. The resort de-
signers had been canny, putting up tall dividers between balconies, tilting the bungalows so that there
was no direct line of sight from one to another. Looking across into the green of palm trees and banana
plants, she had the illusion of complete isolation.

Water dripped down her leg from her soaked clothing and she unbuttoned her shorts absently. As she
was pulling off her tank top, lightning cracked, a gust

of wind blew against her exposed skin, and arousal surged through her.

Suddenly even the wet bikini she wore was too much. She reached back for the clasp. The slider behind her opened with a whish of noise and Dev came out on the deck.

"I see you're getting more comfortable."

God, he was gorgeous, she thought for the hundredth time. His body was like a lean, stripped down machine, not bulky, just full of graceful power. Taylor turned to him and shrugged her shoulders so that the straps of her bikini top fell forward. "I could use some help."

"I'm your man."

"Of course, we need to get you undressed, too," she said, tugging his T-shirt out of his shorts.

"Yes, indeedy." Even as he pulled off the saturated fabric, she had her hands on his bare chest, sliding over the damp skin, brushing at his nipples until they hardened. Dev's breath hissed in. The wet shirt slipped out of his hand and plopped to the balcony floor.

"You'd better get out of those wet shorts, too," she murmured, unzipping them. Impatience gouged at her, impatience to feel him hard and hot in her hand. Impatience to have him hard and hot inside her.

He hooked his fingers in the sides of her bikini bottom and pulled it down slowly over her thighs. When he leaned over and traced the path of his fingers with his tongue, her muscles went weak and she sagged backward into the macramé hammock chair that dangled from the ceiling. Maybe it was the slow swing and turn of the chair that had her feeling giddy, and maybe it was just Dev.

His cock was already hardening as he stood in front of her and she nuzzled it for a moment before she slipped it into her mouth. There was something heady about the taste of him, the feel of him hard against her lips, against her tongue. She felt his fingers stroke her hair, heard his soft groan and she chuckled down in her throat. When she slid him out of her mouth, a translucent pearl of precome oozed out of the tip of him. She reached out with a finger and spread it down and onto the underside, to the silky soft, sensitive spot just below the head where the skin turned darker.

"You wanted a surprise, I think you said," she murmured, looking up at him. "Then maybe you should grab one of those cushions so you can kneel on it."

His eyes looked black, the pupils dilated with desire. He got down on his knees in front of her as she slid to the edge of the hammock chair and hooked her feet over his shoulders. Before she could say anything more, he leaned down and put his mouth against her where she was hot and slick. "No, wait," she managed to say. "I want to…" Her voice trailed off to a soft cry as he went to work with his talented tongue, teasing her, tormenting her in the way that after mere days he'd learned she liked best. Her body tightened with each slick stroke.

Dev raised his head just as she was on the edge of coming. "I'm sorry, I couldn't hear you down there. Did you want me to stop?"

"Please, I want you in me, now," she breathed over the rush of the rain.

"Storm's making too much noise. What was that again?"

"Now," she cried and then he straightened up and

slid into her hard and deep, the rush of it so fast it took her breath away. She felt him, every ridge and vein of him, all the way up inside her until she wanted to scream with it.

Until she wanted more.

Dev locked her legs more securely around his neck, then reached around and tangled his hands in the mesh of the hammock chair. He started her swinging, pulling her toward him and away so that she slid onto his cock then off, on, then off again, hard and deep, deep and fast, every bit of her focused on that one spot, that place where their bodies became one, the center of everything she was about at that instant.

Dev's face was pulled taut with arousal, with the effort of control. Watching his pleasure, being so totally in his control was sending her up and up, coiling the tension in her body. She raised one of her hands to hold her breast, squeezing the nipple until it took her to the edge of the pleasure pain boundary. She slid the other hand across her belly and farther, reaching her finger down to stroke her clitoris every time he slid her away. It was too much, all the sensation, pulling her closer to the edge, closer, closer…

"Taylor, I can't hold on," Dev breathed and then groaned, pulling her hard onto him even as the pleasure flashed through her to her fingers and toes, then back again to her center, sending her quaking and shuddering against him.

5

"WE'RE IN HEAVEN, YOU KNOW." Taylor sat on a cylindrical concrete stool at the swim-up pool bar. Her gaze held a glorious vista of palm trees and golden sand. Warm water lapped about her thighs.

Dev raised his eyebrows. "I'm not sure heaven has a bar." He stood beside her in water up to his waist, resting one arm on the brightly patterned blue tiles of the counter.

"How do you know it doesn't? My idea of heaven is someplace warm and beautiful with no worries and no responsibilities. Maybe this is it." She spun the bright turquoise umbrella from her strawberry daiquiri between her fingers, and leaned over to give him a kiss. "Pinch me."

"Do I get to pick the location?" His eyes were amused as he ran a speculative finger along her collarbone.

"Someplace G-rated," she said. "There are kids playing water polo over there."

He traced a finger down the string that held up the top of her bikini. "They're busy watching the ball," he murmured and drew her away from the bar to lean against the wall of the shoulder-high planter that bowed out from the seating area into the pool. Crimson blossoms of bougainvillea arced out of the planter and hung down over his shoulder as he pulled her against him, his hands warm and sure on her hips.

More and more, he looked like an islander, she thought, with his skin baked dark, his hair caramelized and tousled. She smiled.

"What are you grinning at?"

"You, with your thong necklace and your five-o'clock shadow. You look like you could be a beach bum, living in a thatched hut, catching fish and gathering driftwood."

"There's an idea. And you could sell shells on the beach, help make us a living."

She shook her head. "Nope, I'd do something else, maybe learn how to teach scuba."

The commanding chirp of a whistle had her turning her head. At the water polo net, a brunette wearing the Nova Friends uniform sat in a tall chair and brought order to the game.

Dev gave a low laugh. "Oh, you say you want to teach scuba, but I know what you really dream about doing down here."

"So you've demonstrated," she said, running her hands over his chest.

"Besides that."

She pressed a small kiss on the corner of his mouth. "What else is there?"

"Come on. Admit it."

"What?" The whistle tweeted again and Taylor glanced over to see the brunette laughingly shake her finger at one of the teams.

"You know you want to be a Nova Friend," he laughed, pointing to the referee.

"Oh, please."

"Admit it. I see you stare at them when they're on

stage in the nightclub act. You want to wear silver lame and lip synch to Madonna, too.''

"You know me so well," she said dryly.

He tipped his head to the side modestly. "So it's settled. We'll stay here. You can sell shells during the day and Raoul will help you become a Nova Friend by night. I'll be your groupie and beach bum."

Taylor shot him a suspicious look. "Wait a minute. How come I have to work and you get to lie around on the beach?"

"Well, I'm going to be your boy toy. That takes work, you know. I'll need to conserve my strength."

"Don't start conserving it yet," she murmured, stepping in against him. "We've got days." Time stopped at the touch of mouth against mouth, slippery skin against skin. How could he call her insatiable? Touching him wasn't a choice, it was a biological need, like air, or water.

A scream shivered the air and they jerked apart. Taylor's head snapped around as she searched for the source. The beach? The dive pool? The lunch palapa? The scream came again.

"What the...?" she heard Dev say and realized that he wasn't looking across the pool or toward the restaurant or toward any of the places she was.

He was looking straight up.

Above them, her legs dangling from the harness that suspended her bright yellow chute, was a parasailer. Perhaps the tow boat had come in too close to shore, perhaps it had merely been a sudden gust of wind that had carried her up over the beach, but now she hung above their heads, over the pool and thatch-roofed bar, over the buildings of the resort. She shrieked again, even as the boat towing her headed out to sea, raising her up higher, pulling her out to safety.

"People are out of their minds."

"For what, parasailing?"

She nodded.

He slipped his hands back around her waist. "A lot of people think it's fun."

"Sure, as long as you're not getting spitted on a beach umbrella."

"They got her away safely," he pointed out.

Taylor turned to watch the sail again, as he'd seen her watch it over the past days when they were on the beach.

"Have you ever tried it?" he asked.

She shook her head. "No. I think I'd feel kind of silly, paying to just hang there and hope I don't fall."

"You should try it," he suggested. "It's a rush. Anyway, I thought you were a woman who lived life on the edge, dropping top in public and all that."

"Dropping top doesn't cost me $50."

His teeth gleamed. "Depends on where you do it."

"Are you going to make a citizen's arrest?" she asked, looking at him from under her lashes.

"I left my cuffs at home."

She leaned in for a kiss. "Too bad," she murmured, her lips against his.

"Seriously, though," he said between kisses, "if you don't think it looks like fun, that's a reason not to do it. But not because you think it looks silly or because it costs too much. When are you going to have a chance to do this again?"

"Next time I'm down here on vacation."

"And you said this was your first vacation in what, five years?"

"And I don't want it to be my last," she said firmly. "Let's go back to the beach."

"All right." He set their empty cups on the bar and led her toward the steps on the far side of the pool, skirting the water polo game. In the center, the fountain sent a spray of droplets dancing on the water.

Climbing out of the water must feel like leaving the moon to come back to Earth gravity, he thought. The concrete of the poolside was hot under his bare feet.

"And even if parasailing is silly," he said, linking his fingers with hers. "What do you have that's more meaningful to do?"

"I can think of a thing or two." She gave him a bawdy leer that had him laughing.

"Are you propositioning me?"

Taylor adjusted her sun hat and gave him a side-long glance. "Me?" she said demurely. "Surely you must be mistaken."

"Looks like I'll have to take you in after all, ma'am," he said firmly, turning down one of the side footpaths that led back to the huts. "Come on."

"What's the charge, officer?" she asked, trotting along behind him.

"I'll think of something."

"I can hardly wait."

"I CAN'T DECIDE IF I LIKE playing with you better in your room or in my room," Taylor said lazily as she lay on the bed watching Dev pull on his swim trunks.

"Just remember, if you want to keep me as your boy toy, you'll have to go to work to support me," he said, picking her bikini bottoms off the television where they had landed when she'd thrown them off.

"Oh right, as a Nova Friend," she said slipping on the scrap of turquoise lycra and standing up to stretch. "You just want to see me doing a shimmy onstage."

"I'd rather have a private show."

"It'll cost you," she warned. "I'll expect service in return."

He pulled her to him.

"Maybe a trade," she murmured, sighing at the feel of his lips. How could it be that she never tired of it, of him? He could heat her up with a word, a look. He could have her laughing until her sides hurt. He could soothe her, reading to her while she lay with her head in his lap, with his hand playing over her hair. They'd been inseparable for the past five days, yet all she wanted was more. If it hadn't been a vacation fling, with a clear time frame and a clear end, she'd have been nervous.

Taking a breath, Taylor made herself let him go. Definitely time to get out on the beach before she began taking it all seriously.

She was bending over to pick up her bikini top when she heard a string of beeps as Dev unlocked the electronic safe in the closet. "What are you doing?" she asked, fighting to hook her clasp behind her as he extracted a sheaf of pesos.

"I need to spend these." He reached back into the closet to lock the safe.

"What on earth are you going to spend it on? It's an all-inclusive resort, remember?"

"Not everything is included."

"What, souvenirs?" She straightened her shoulder straps.

"Nope."

"Magazines?"

He tucked the cash into the pocket of his swim trunks. "Nope."

"A snorkeling trip?" she asked, putting on her sunglasses.

"Nope."

"What, then?"

"I'm going to take you parasailing," he said, and kissed the tip of her nose.

THE CLASP OF THE PARASAILING harness snicked into place. Taylor stood on the back deck of the parasail boat, equal parts excitement and alarm shivering through her. "This was all your idea, you know," she said to Dev. "If I get killed or maimed, it'll be all your fault. My family will blame you when I'm in the hospital."

"Well, you do have travel insurance, don't you?"

"Don't even start with me," she said with a laugh.

In front of her stood the pedestal that reeled out the cable that would—she fervently hoped—tie her to the boat. Taylor gripped the line as the boat started to move. The boat assistant, barefoot and wearing a Señor Frog's baseball cap, picked up the chute off the deck so the breeze from the boat's passage could get inside. It drifted through her mind that this really wasn't a good idea, not a good idea at all.

Then she felt it, the first jolt of wind, like a giant hand tugging her backward. Her feet rose off the deck of the boat for a moment and she gave a sudden whoop of surprised laughter. The sound of the engine rose as they gathered speed. The wind caught and held this time and suddenly it was pulling her up and up, the line unspooling from the boat as she went.

Her cry of jubilation was the same one that roller

coasters had drawn from her as an adolescent. Speed, motion, the rush of wind past her ears, it all blended together to put her senses in a whirl. Flying must feel this way, she thought, this sense of being buoyed up by the air, skimming through it effortlessly.

As she rose up, she stared at the beauty below her, the glowing blue of the water, the lush green of the jungle, the thatched roofs of the resort buildings looking like a club of witches had tossed down their hats and gone for a swim. The waves glittered below; ahead, in the distance, she saw the majestic white of a cruise ship.

Taylor laughed aloud, seized by exhilaration. She didn't ever want to come down. What a gift, to soar, to fly. What a gift to feel this way. And who had given it to her? She looked down to the boat below and saw Dev looking back at her, and she waved. His hand moved to his mouth and he blew her a kiss.

"THAT WAS ONE OF THE MOST amazing experiences I've ever had," Taylor said as they swam in the ocean in the afternoon sun.

"See? Snorkeling, parasailing, you ought to listen to me when I suggest things. Aren't you glad I pushed you into it?" Two years spent with his ex-fiancée and her moods had nearly made him forget that uncomplicated pleasure existed. Being with Taylor was simply a delight.

She splashed water at him. "It's not nice to be smug."

He dropped down to duck under the water and came back up, shaking his wet hair out of his eyes. "I like watching you have fun," he said, scooping her against him.

"I haven't had this good a time in too long to re-member."

"You know what they say, all work and no play," he said, putting his hands on her rib cage and lifting her so she could wrap her legs around his waist. Her breasts bobbled on the surface of the water.

"I don't know. I lost the trick of it somehow." She shrugged and he saw the flash of shadows in her eyes. "This whole week has been like finding a part of me I'd lost."

Dev frowned, then he made himself release it. Not his problem, he reminded himself. "This is what you were made for," he said, sliding his hands over her hips. "Trying out adventures, feeling good."

"I could just do this for months, lie around the beach all day, play in the water."

"I'm telling you, all you have to do is join the Nova Friends. I'll build the beach shack and we'll be all set."

Taylor linked her arms around his neck. "There are terms to that deal, don't forget."

He eyed her. "Your point?"

She leaned in toward him, brushing her tongue tip over his lips, featherlight. "You're supposed to be my boy toy, aren't you?"

"It's a tough job, but somebody's got to do it." He reached out a hand and cupped her breast.

"Mmm. Careful."

"There's no one else near us and we're too far from the beach for anyone to see." Out here by the string of floating corks, away from the dive dock, the water was peaceful, deserted. He felt the firm swell of her breast under his fingers. Taylor caught her breath and shifted against him and he felt himself harden at her heat, her softness.

The slow pressure of the swells pressed against them.

The touch of his palm on the sensitive flesh felt outrageously provocative as he traced the outside of her breast. It teased, it aroused, it made her want.

Taylor moistened her lips. ''Maybe we should go in and see if we can do anything about that.''

''Or maybe we should do it right here,'' he said softly.

''But...'' she sputtered, trying not to move against his fingers as they stroked her breasts. ''There's a beach full of people out there.''

''They can't see what we're doing.''

''What if someone comes in the water?''

''Besides us?'' he said with a wicked smile. ''We could see them long before they get here. Come on, you've seen all the honeymooners out here wrapped together before. What did you think they were doing?''

His mouth was warm on her neck, his fingers pressed at her nipple. Desire burst through her. What would it be like to make love, to have an orgasm under the brilliance of the tropical sky, while a beach full of people lay a hundred yards away? It was an outrageous thing to try to get away with, she thought, as her breath came quicker.

Abruptly there was nothing she wanted more.

''I'll just say two words,'' Dev murmured. ''Snorkeling. Parasailing.''

''I'm sold.''

The scent of him blended with that of the ocean. The stubble of his chin contrasted with the softness of his lips as they traveled over her cheek and down her neck, journeying back to claim her mouth with a speed and force that left her breathless.

He groaned at the combination of sensations, her breasts filling his hands, the soft heat of her against his growing erection. He pulled her back to him. "Have you ever made love before in the out-of-doors, in public?" he murmured, running a hand down the flat of her belly to slide under the edge of her suit bottom as his mouth came back to claim hers. Then his fingers slid lower, passing curls of hair to plunge abruptly into a hot slickness that nearly made him explode.

Taylor jolted in shock, then strained against him with a stifled moan as he started to stroke that firm, slippery nubbin hidden in its private folds. And all sensation coalesced into that one point. The contrast between friction and slickness had her strung tight with tension. She swayed her hips unconsciously, moving with the water, moving against his touch. Then he plunged his fingers inside her and suddenly she was being carried along by a surge of pleasure that swept her up, up, up and over to float down, as she'd floated in the sky from the parasail.

She caught her breath, gasping a little in the aftermath, conscious once again of the warm water, the beach, the people.

The people.

The tension had abated. The arousal hadn't. If anything, it was stronger. "So you want to make love under the open sky?" she whispered. "You want to come in me when a hundred people are watching?" Her fingers slipped lower, teasing loose the string that bound his trunks. She could feel the heat and hardness of him, feel him jerking against her touch. Impatiently she pushed the suit down his hips and then she had him in her hand, silky soft and rock hard, the velvety tip just a bit slippery. It was intoxicating, the touch, the texture, the shudder and jerk.

Dev groaned and stilled her hand, holding himself in check by the barest thread as he put his hands on her ribs and raised her in the water so that she could position him. Then he plunged into her in a single fierce thrust.

Tight, hot heat gripped him, dizzying in its intensity. Her legs wrapped around him like silken bonds, and for an instant he didn't dare move, sure if he did, it would end there and then. Seconds passed, punctuated only by shuddering breaths. Then he felt her tighten around him and he began to shift her body up and down in the buoyant water, sliding himself in and out of her. "Look at the beach, darlin'," he murmured. "Look up at the sky."

It was intoxicating, the contrast of openness and the intimacy of having his cock hard and deep inside her. The texture, the pressure, the slippery friction all blended into a single physical rush as she clutched helplessly at his shoulders, moaning with the pleasure. She lay back onto the water, arms floating free now, linked to him only by her legs around his waist, his hardness embedded deep inside her. The cool of the water contrasted with the heat from his body. A creature of pure sensation, she felt his hands on her hips, sliding her body up and down, thrusting himself into her hard and deep.

Dev watched her gasp with the intensity of what she felt. How was it that watching her quake with it was more exciting to him than even what his own body felt? Holding himself on the thin edge of reason, he drank in the feeling, the texture, the scents, savoring the flavor of her still on his lips. He pulled her back up toward him and wrapped her arms around his neck, capturing her mouth to lay claim, devour.

They moved together urgently, climbing higher and higher with each stroke. Suddenly every sensation intensified as she felt him thicken, grow harder still as he approached his peak.

"Look at the beach, look at the people." His voice was taut and mesmerizing.

Taylor's eyes widened as she rubbed against him one last time, then in the next stroke she was shuddering, crying out as the climax gripped her, tightening down to a pinpoint then flaring throughout her body like a shower of sparks.

Driven past control by the smoothness, the heat, her contractions clenching around him, Dev followed her over the edge, swaying to and fro. Then a wave came along, bigger than the rest, and they toppled into the salty water.

6

"WAKE UP, GORGEOUS."

Taylor opened her eyes in the morning dimness of the room to see Dev lying next to her, already in a T-shirt and swim trunks. "Forget it," she mumbled, burrowing into her pillow. "I'm on vacation."

"Come on," he coaxed, pressing kisses on her neck. "It's our last day, I don't want to waste it."

She rolled over to look up at him. "Come back to bed and get naked. I guarantee we won't waste it."

"That's a tempting offer." He leaned in and kissed her until her head was spinning.

What a person would do for this rush of desire, she thought, curving a hand around the back of his neck.

Then he straightened up, taking the pillow and sheet with him.

She yelped at the sudden theft. "Savage," she muttered.

"Come and get it," he invited, backing toward the bathroom with her pillow in his hands.

"You're an evil man, Dev Carson." She shot him a sulky look. Finally, though, she gave into the inevitable and got up.

"I've got your best interests at heart."

She stood at the bathroom counter groping for her toothbrush. "My best interests involve sleeping in."

"You just don't know what's good for you. Too

much sleeping in just makes you tired. Trust me, you'll thank me for this later.''

"Hah," she sputtered through a mouth of toothpaste. When he stepped behind her and filled his hands with her breasts, she swatted at him.

"Sorry. You just looked like you were losing your balance and I wanted to help."

She dried her face and put the toothbrush away. "You can help me back to bed," she suggested silkily.

"How about if I inspect your dental hygiene, instead," he offered, scooping her in close and closing his mouth on hers.

Okay, so there were some things worth getting up for, Taylor thought driftingly, as the dart and stroke and heat of his tongue sent shivers through her. It amazed her afresh every time, the way he could sweep her into single-minded desire, the way it was never enough, even though they'd been together virtually every minute since her first day on the island.

"Back to bed," she murmured.

"Oh, no," Dev countered, turning her around and urging her toward the shower with a little slap on her behind. "I've got something special planned."

"It would be even more special if it involved bed."

He considered. "Maybe a nap, later."

"Is that the best you can do?"

He fought a grin. "'Fraid so."

Breakfast improved her outlook enough that she felt almost human as they walked out to the beach. "You haven't signed us up for some all-day dive, have you?" she asked suspiciously.

"Nothing that's nearly such hard work," he assured her, ducking under the nodding fronds of a palm tree. Instead of heading to their usual palapa, though, he turned toward the end of the beach where the sports equipment lay.

The sand was golden, the sky was clear, and the water stretched away in a hundred shades of aquamarine. What more did they need than this, Taylor thought.

"*Hola, Miguel,*" Dev said, waving to the lithe teenager who signed out the sea kayaks and jet skis to guests.

"*Hola, señor. Como estas?*"

"*Bien. Et tu?*"

"*Bien, tambien.* Your accent, it is much better, Señor Dev."

"I've had a good teacher, Miguel."

They did a complicated handshake, the teenager grinning delightedly when it was through. "Your handshaking is much better, *señor,* also."

"All due to you, Señor Miguel. So is the boat ready?"

"*Si.*"

Dev turned to Taylor. "This is Miguel. He handles all the sailboats and board surfers here. He knows the water around the island like no one else. Miguel, this is Señorita Taylor. Taylor, this is my buddy Miguel."

They shook hands, the boy glancing at her with liquid, dark eyes, then looking down bashfully. "And the *señorita, amigo,* she is going to sail with you also?"

"I can't leave her here with you, Miguel. You'd smile at her and steal her away."

The boy blushed.

"Any foul weather coming today?"

"The weather, she is fine, *señor.* Maybe little rain

later.'' He led the way past the surfing boards and rack of life vests to an orange-sailed catamaran that sat beyond the other craft.

It was a bit bigger than the usual Hobie Cats that hotel guests sailed off the beach, its sail striped in a sunburst of red and orange. She'd never seen it out on the water that she recalled. Taylor watched, bemused, as her shoes, shorts, towel and beach bag disappeared into waterproof compartments in the hulls. Then Dev and Miguel pushed it down the sand to the water, pushing it in until it was bobbing gently.

''Okay, hop on,'' Dev said, patting the blue webbing trampoline that stretched between the twin hulls.

''*Hasta la vista, amigos,*'' Miguel called and gave a push.

Taylor felt the moment the breeze caught the sail. Suddenly, instead of skimming slowly over the water, the boat was alive under them and they were heading out toward the open water.

The sea spread out around them smooth and blue, so vivid that it hurt the eyes. Dev sent them along the coast at a slight angle, adjusted the tiller almost absently as they rose and fell with the swells. From their vantage point, Cozumel was a paradise lined with palm trees and palapas, and the occasional neon-sailed board surfer.

Surprisingly quickly, the tame landscape of the resort gave way to rough coastline, and the weather-worn structures of an abandoned beach club.

''Okay, I give. Where are we going?'' Even with the light breeze, it was easy to hear.

Dev smiled. ''I thought I'd show you the other side of the island, get away from the Iberonova for a while. There are some Mayan ruins over there you might like.''

It did feel good to get away from the hermetically sealed environment of the resort, Taylor realized. There was a freedom to being out on the water with the wind in her face that she'd never expected. Out on the water, a person could breath.

In the distance, a trio of cruisers clustered together. She tapped Dev's shoulder and pointed. ''What's over there?''

Dev glanced over. ''Dive boats at Palancar Reef. A little farther south is Columbia Reef, where we went snorkeling.''

''Is that where we're going now?''

He shook his head. ''Southeast. We'll head around the bottom of the island and come up the other side for a bit. Right now, though, we're going to need to tack or we're going to be heading to the mainland,'' he said, adjusting the sail. ''When I say go, move to the other side of the trampoline. Be careful of the sail. I'll hand you the lines and you just pull until the sail anchors come across to you. Ready?''

Taylor nodded, getting up on her hands and feet. ''Go.''

Like a spider, she scuttled across the trampoline to a spot on the other hull of the cat. The assembly slid smoothly across to her with just a tug even as Dev shifted across with the tiller. Exultant laughter bubbled to her lips as she felt the wind bring the boat around to point toward Cozumel again.

''Good job,'' Dev said, grinning at her.

''This is great. I've never been sailing before,'' she said, turning her face into the breeze. ''Have you done it long?''

"Oh, Miguel gave me a couple of pointers last week," he said blandly, then laughed when she gave a startled glance to the coastline, which suddenly seemed very far away. "Relax, I've been sailing for years."

"Just as long as you can get us back," she said, giving him a suspicious look.

"You know how to swim, don't you?"

She gave his shoulder a push. "I thought you said this was a no work day, although you had to be lying through your pearly white teeth. I've seen photos, aren't you supposed to hang off the side of these things or something to keep them from tipping over?"

"That's mostly when you're in rough weather or trying to really fill your sails," he said easily. "I'll show you. Hold on," he said and shifted the tiller a bit.

The hull that they sat on jumped out of the water. Taylor gave an involuntary yelp and grabbed a handhold before Dev turned the boat and brought her back in contact with the water.

"Relax."

"I am relaxed. I was just surprised."

His teeth gleamed. "Don't worry, I'll warn you next time. Anyway, it's so calm around here you hardly need to worry about it unless you're trying to go fast."

"Maybe I want to go fast."

Dev gave her a speculative look. "Who knows, maybe we'll strap you on and hang you over the side when we go around the bottom of the island. The winds might get tricky down there."

"Sounds like fun," she said, squinting across to the tiny knot of buildings on the mainland that was the town of Playa del Carmen. ''So how'd you get into sailing? Did you learn it as a kid?''

''I lived in Newport for a while. A buddy of mine was into sailing and dragged me out on the water until I got hooked.''

Taylor watched his sure hand on the tiller. ''Were you a hard sell?''

''Not very,'' he admitted.

''I suspected as much. So do you have a boat?''

He nodded. ''Not very big. Just enough to take out on the Chesapeake on a nice day. I'll take you out some time when we get home, if you like,'' he said idly, watching the water ahead of them.

She almost agreed without thinking, then froze. Where was her head at? Keep it safe, keep it loose. The last thing she needed to do was get involved with a man on the rebound, however appealing that man might be. ''The deal is, it's over when we leave here, remember?''

He hesitated, his eyes masked behind his dark glasses. ''Right. Time to tack again,'' he said briskly.

By the time they'd switched sides and shifted the sail, the moment had passed.

They headed south along a Cozumel coastline very different than it had been earlier. Gone were the resorts, or indeed, nearly all signs of humans. Now it was rugged and wild. Coconut palms, mangrove and palmetto edged the island shore. It felt intimate, somehow, to be seeing these places with Dev alone, as though they were castaways with only each other to turn to.

She watched a pelican fly low along the water, as graceful in flight as it was ungainly on the ground. It dove into the ocean with a splash, only to emerge with a wriggling fish in its bill. She leaned in to kiss Dev.

He glanced at her. "What was that for?"

"Thank you for doing this," she said simply. "It's really lovely."

"I thought you might like it." He ran his hand up and down her back.

"What's that?" she asked, pointing to a knob of white that had appeared farther down the coast.

"A lighthouse. Built at the turn of the century. It's a museum now."

"Did you come here with Raoul?"

Dev nodded. "He took me around the island a couple of weeks ago. Showed me a good place for lunch. Time to tack."

They shifted sides again, this time smoothly.

"You and Raoul have become buddies."

"He's a good guy. You know he's lived here most of his life, except when he was in school on the mainland? He knows this island inside out. When we were sailing around, he was pointing out trees that he's watched grow from when he was a kid." There was a trace of envy in Dev's voice.

"You sound like you want that."

"I think it would make you a different kind of person, to be that close to the place you lived. It would make you rooted, you know? I feel like I've always been on the move."

"Why don't you stop, then?" she asked curiously.

He shrugged. "It's never seemed like the right time before. But I've been thinking about it a lot lately. My fiancée wanted to move to Florida and I hated the idea."

"Doesn't sound too practical if you're a business owner."

He gave a quick grimace. "Melissa was never much on practical. One of the many ways we didn't mix. But that's a story I won't bore you with."

They sailed past the lighthouse, which stood tall and white. The wind freshened. There was a rumble in the distance.

"Okay, we're going to come about. Grab that harness there and buckle it on," he directed, following suit. "That'll let you swing out over the side without coming off. It's time to have a little fun with the trapeze."

Even as Taylor was buckling on the harness, the hull was bouncing on the surface of the water, then rising up.

"First we tack so that we can come about."

Abruptly the motion of the boat turned even more active. "Okay," Dev said, "let's take advantage of this wind and see what this baby can really do."

An unholy buzz of excitement rose in her.

"Now sit on the edge," he directed, fastening on his own harness. "When you start to feel the hull come up, lean back until you feel it stabilize."

Taylor slid back and leaned out, only open space behind her. Gradually the rising motion stopped until they were skidding along on one hull, the other hovering a foot off the water. Taylor whooped exuberantly.

"Having fun?" Dev asked with a grin.

"What do you think?"

"I think we should step it up a bit." He adjusted the tiller and suddenly they were skimming over the

waves, sitting four or five feet above the water, the
wind raking through their hair.

The landscape had become steadily more wild,
rocky in places, overgrown with vegetation in others.
In contrast to the calm of the other coast, the sea had
become choppy with little whitecaps, waves that had
traveled all the way across the Atlantic ocean from
Africa.

"Is it always so rough along here?"

Dev shook his head. "It's never as quiet as the
other coast, but it wasn't this bad the other day when
I was out with Raoul. I think we have a squall coming
in." Indeed, now that they were tacking back toward
the island, she saw the threatening clouds massed up
in the sky, surging over from the mainland. It was the
daily cloudburst, something that she normally ignored. Now, though, out on the open water and un-
protected, she found herself flooded with adrenaline.

Lightning forked down.

"Dev," she shouted.

"I know. We need to get on shore and wait this
out."

"Can we? It looks rocky."

"There's a little cove up here that Raoul pointed
out to me. We should have time to get to it and beat
the clouds."

By the time they reached the cove, the rain had
begun, heavy drops thumping down around them.
Taylor felt it sluicing through her hair as they dragged
the boat onto the beach, out of reach of the waves.
No shy pitter-pattering here in the tropics. When the
sun shone, it did so with a vengeance, and when it
rained, likewise. None of the palms that dotted the
beach was going to be much help to them.

With a crack like a gunshot, lightning arced down ahead of them, making her jump. "Get down," Dev roared, yanking her onto the sand. She felt him pressed against her, wet and warm, and she was tempted to laugh until the hairs on her arms started to tingle and raise up. Static charge, she realized with thudding heart, and she opened her mouth to warn Dev.

With a blinding flash and an earsplitting crack, a yellow bolt shot down to hit the top of a palm no more than twenty feet away from them. Alarm lunged through her. Though she knew that staying flat was the best thing she could do, every instinct in her body told her to run for cover. Instead she trembled.

ANOTHER BOLT OF LIGHTNING cracked down in the jungle behind them and Dev pressed himself harder against Taylor, as though his body could somehow protect her from the millions of volts of electricity that might flood down from the sky at any instant. He cursed himself for getting so preoccupied with her and the sheer joy of sailing that he hadn't kept an eye out for the squall. If he'd timed it better, they might have gotten under cover. As it was, all they could do was wait it out.

Wind rattled the palm fronds nearby. Behind them the sea boiled and seethed. He wanted them out on an open beach. They shouldn't be near anything tall like a palm in a lightning storm, but raising up at this point was a bigger risk.

The hairs on his arms prickled again and he said a silent prayer. This time, the bolt exploded so close it sounded like it was on top of them. With a crack, most of the top of the palm closest to them split off,

thudding down on the sand nearby. The sharpness of
ozone filled the air.

And in sudden shock, he felt himself getting hard.

Now that was sick. Here they were stranded in a
lightning storm where they could be hit any minute,
and he was thinking about that soft, springy body under his, thinking about the way she was shifting herself against him. She was probably terrified and all he
could think about was how good it would feel to drive
himself into her tight heat. Her eyes weren't closed,
he realized as he stared down into her face. They were
staring at him, bright with…not fear, he realized, nor
alarm, but…excitement?

Then she curved a hand around his neck and pulled
his mouth down hard on hers.

The rain came down in earnest, peppering his back
with a thousand tiny blows. And yet he barely registered it, conscious only of the wet and willing
woman underneath him. Her lips were avid, greedy.
She nipped at his mouth, and the needlelike instant
of pain only sent desire flaring in its wake. Alarm at
the storm was forgotten. Thundering, pulsing through
him was the unbearable compulsion to drive himself
into her, to pour himself into that heat, that softness.

Taylor dragged Dev's shirt over his head, not caring if she ripped it, craving skin under her palms, the
ropy play of muscles under her fingers. It was life,
urgency, need that flowed back and forth between
them. Rain poured down in sheets. The sky lit with
lightning, silhouetting him, making his eyes ghostly
pale for a moment.

He dragged off her bikini bottoms, and moved back
up over her; she raked her nails down his back. Gen-
tleness was only a memory. There was no time for

foreplay and none was needed. The storm played on some primitive part of both of them and they were more ready than either had ever been before.

When he slid into her, it was hard and deep, and so fast it took her breath away. Her cry was sharp, even as she wrapped her legs around his waist. They took each other tooth and claw, each flash of pleasure, each flash of pain a reminder that they were alive in the fury of the storm.

And when they tumbled into orgasm together, their exultant cries echoed against the background of the thunder.

TAYLOR LAY BACK, PILLOWING her head on Dev's stomach. His hand stroked her cheek.

"There's lunch in the cooler in the hull," he said.

"When I can move, maybe."

Sunlight shone down through the dissipating clouds. One minute the fury of the storm, the next, golden calm. This was weather in the tropics.

"The boat made it through okay, right?" Taylor asked.

"We got lucky."

"I'll say," she said, giving a contented laugh.

"I'll say one thing, sailing with you beats the hell out of sailing with Raoul."

"I should hope so." She pulled off her sunglasses and looked at the play of sunlight and clouds. "Are we going to run into trouble going home?"

"I don't see why. The storm's over. We can hang out for a couple of hours and eat or head on up the coast, either way. As long as we start for home a couple of hours before dusk, we'll be perfect."

"It's perfect right now." It was, she thought, lying

with Dev's hand in her hair, the sun beginning to shine warm on her, and the regular rhythm of his breath pillowing her head. She didn't want it to end. Longing tugged at her. She wasn't ready to give this up, not just the lazy days, but the passion, the companionship, the laughter, the adventure.

A sudden bolt of alarm hit her. Oh, no, she thought. This wasn't about a vacation fling or a physical affair. This was something much more dangerous, this tug. Flings didn't feel this good, and nothing that felt this good came without a price. Dev Carson was on the rebound. Anyway, however much she might feel as if she knew him after they'd spent every moment together in the past week, she didn't. She, of all people, had reason to appreciate that you never really knew anyone.

"Are you okay?" Dev asked. "You just jumped."

"I was just dozing off," she lied, even as every muscle in her body screamed to flee. She hadn't feared the waves on the ocean before they'd landed. She hadn't feared the lightning. Despite the obvious danger, both had filled her with a strange exhilaration.

This is what she feared.

It was okay, she reasoned. When she woke up the next morning, it would be over. Twenty-four hours from now, she'd be on a plane, safe, flying home. She'd never see him again.

A long-term thing? He didn't want it, she didn't want it. Everything they wanted from each other they'd found in the physical connection. Anything else was just foolishness, confusing sex with something more. She'd known the man for a week. Okay, so maybe they'd been together nearly every moment of that week, maybe the time translated into months of dating, but it was only a fling.

Nothing more.

7

IT WAS RIDICULOUS TO FEEL down, Dev thought as he watched the orange and white airport shuttle pull away from the front of the resort. That shuttle was carrying Taylor away from him. He could still taste her on his lips, could still remember the way it had felt to wake with her that morning.

Still, it was over. Probably for the best, he told himself as he turned back to the open air lobby with its lush central planter open to the sky and its whistling macaws. Definitely for the best. After all, it was what they had agreed to in the beginning. It had been a great week—a dream week—but it was time to get back to real life.

He'd just gotten out of one relationship. The last thing he needed to do was jump into another. That would be bad for both of them. Best to do the smart thing and consign the whole fling to his personal history book.

And he was so full of shit, he thought to himself sardonically, if he figured for one minute that he could go back to Baltimore and stay away from her.

"*Hola, amigo.*" A hand clapped him on the shoulder and he turned to find Raoul. They shook hands in a thumbs-up clasp. "Tomorrow is your last day, eh?"

Dev nodded. "Got to go back to work."

"You should move down here, my friend. If you

worked at the Iberonova, you could stay always in paradise.''

The problem was that without Taylor, it wasn't really paradise anymore.

"And the *señorita*," Raoul gave him a knowing look, "does she go back with you?"

Dev frowned and shook his head. "No. She just left for home."

"Ah. No wonder the long face, *amigo*. But you will see her again. You live in the same town, no?"

A smile tugged at the corners of his mouth. "Well, yeah, but it's a little bigger than San Miguel," he said, referring to Cozumel's tiny village. "We probably won't run into each other on the street."

Raoul gave him an amused glance. "In my country, a smart man does not leave such things to chance. She is a very lovely woman, the *señorita*. The sort who might be hard to forget."

"She is a very stubborn woman, also."

"Ah." His eyes lit. "The very best kind. A challenge, yes, but a prize worth winning." He kissed his fingertips and flicked them outward.

Dev stared at him. Raoul looked back steadily. Finally Dev laughed. "Do you know everything, Raoul?"

He gave a modest shrug. "Only that which is worth knowing, amigo."

TAYLOR STARED OUT THE WINDOW of the plane, watching the serene blue of the Gulf of Mexico pass away beneath her. She shifted in her seat and the twinge of sore muscles from her inner thighs had her thinking again about Dev. As though she'd stopped thinking of him for a moment since the taxi had pulled away from the resort. Or since she'd first seen him on the beach a week before, for that matter.

Of course, it wasn't leaving him behind that had her wistful. It was just normal end-of-vacation blues. She wouldn't think about how good it had felt to hold on to him, she wouldn't think about his soft mouth and those callused hands that could make her shiver just brushing across her arm. She specifically wouldn't think about how it had felt to fall asleep with him, to feel him press a sleepy kiss to her hair when she turned over in his arms.

He probably drank straight out of the milk carton and left his dirty socks on the bathroom floor, she told herself sternly. No doubt if they'd been together for more than a week he would have driven her crazy. Definitely, the magic would have worn off.

No, the week was over—and with it, their arrangement. It was just as well, really. It had been luscious and memorable, but she had no intention of walking back into a relationship. Just the idea of it gave her the willies.

"Something to drink for you?"

Taylor glanced up to see the flight attendant looking at her expectantly. "Please," she said. "I'll have…" A smile bloomed across her face. "I'll have a shot of tequila with a lime."

Like postcards, images from the week just past flashed in her mind, the iguana that walked out of the foliage a foot from her toes and disappeared in a stand of palmettos, the school of gray and cobalt fish that had surrounded her when they'd dived the reef, the hermit crabs that she'd watched totter down the beach carrying their oversized whorled shells.

She reached in her pocket and brought out a tiny

pointed shell that Dev had pressed into her hand as she waited for the shuttle. "A memory of Cozumel," he'd said.

And the glow of memory went through her to her toes.

"Okay, here we go, one tequila," the flight attendant said, setting the glass at her elbow.

Taylor picked it up and held it up to the window. Watching the water of the Gulf slide away below, she made a mental toast to Mexico, to vacation flings, and most of all to Dev Carson. It had been nice while it lasted.

THE BRUSHED STEEL PANELS of the baggage carousel clacked as Taylor stood waiting for her bag, staring with distaste at the wool coat and scarf she held. If there was no bliss like escaping the howling chill of winter to the sleepy heat of the Caribbean, there was no shock like the return. She struggled to forget the fact that twenty-four hours before she'd been dancing under the stars in a spaghetti strapped mini dress and sandals.

Dancing in Dev's arms.

"Stop it," she said aloud.

"This isn't a good sign," said a voice behind her. "You go to the Caribbean for three weeks and you come back talking to yourself? I told you that you should have taken me along."

Taylor turned to see a woman wearing a red wool beret over a wealth of dark, curly hair. The beret matched her red lips and rosy cheeks, not to mention her vivid red cape. Taylor grinned at her and stepped in for a tired hug.

She and Jody Bradshaw had been college roommates together at Brown, traveling the sometimes bumpy road to adulthood. But it was the road they'd traveled since that time that had truly cemented their friendship. It had been long and fraught with peril, but they had managed it.

"Welcome home. You look disgustingly tanned and healthy. I'm going to call my travel agent."

"I am your travel agent."

"Well, get to work and book me to Mexico, already." Jody eyed her. "How was it, anyway?"

"It was a great vacation. It's just the eight hours of airplanes and airports that wear me out."

"Gee, and here I was hoping it was a gorgeous man with an inexhaustible sex drive."

"That, too," Taylor told her.

Jody stared at her. "You? Ms. Pure As A Nun? Now this I gotta hear."

"Trust me, I'll—" Taylor broke off as she spied her bag sailing serenely. She followed it for a few frantic steps before wrestling it off the carousel.

"I still don't understand how you can be gone for a week and only take a garment bag," Jody said, taking Taylor's computer bag. "I take more than that for a weekend."

"Remember, I'm the one who gives seminars on packing for your vacation. Besides, you know hot weather clothes take up less space than sweaters and snow boots," Taylor added. She stopped near the door and gave a baleful glance at her heavy wool coat.

"You'd better bite the bullet," Jody advised. "It's about twenty-five degrees out there. Welcome home, pookums."

Taylor pulled the coat on and wrapped her scarf around her neck, stifling the groan.

"So tell me about your vacation and loafing, I mean working, while you visited all those resorts," Jody said, taking the garment bag and heading toward the parking garage. "At least one of us should have had a good time."

"Hey, it's been over five years for me. I had it coming."

"I'll say. So tell me about him."

"Let's see." She pretended to think. "His name was Dev. He had a gorgeous body, a fabulous mouth, eyes you could dive into." The sudden twinge of longing she felt took her by surprise. "He was sexy, funny, with these amazing shoulders—" her hands fluttered in the air to shape them "—eyes you could swim in…"

"You're repeating yourself," Jody said dryly.

"His eyes deserve it."

"What color?"

"Sea-green, like drift glass."

Jody drew to a halt in front of her car. "I can just imagine. So where does he live, Peoria?"

"Not exactly."

"Salt Lake City?"

Taylor rolled her eyes. "Um, around here, I think."

Jody goggled at her. "You're kidding, right?"

Taylor shook her head as she put her bag in the trunk.

"Oh, that's too perfect. Not only do you have a vacation fling, but you get to keep going."

"No way," Taylor said emphatically. "It was a just for fun thing, but that's it."

"What are you talking about?" Jody exclaimed

over the roof of the car before she got in. "This guy sounds like a god. You guys have already gotten together. There is no way you're telling me that you don't want to find him and start right back up with where you were."

Taylor snapped on her seat belt. "Jody, the last thing I want is to get caught up in a relationship. We had a fling and it was fun, but that's that."

"Taylor, you just spent a week eating each other alive. Why not see him a few times?"

Taylor huffed impatiently. "Neither one of us wants it. He just got hung out to dry by his fiancée. I need to be the guy's rebound woman like I need a hole in the head. Besides, I might have spent the week playing with him, but I'm still not too man crazy myself."

"Sounds like you were crazy about him for a bit, though."

"Why not? We were on vacation, there weren't any rules. Why not run with it?" She brushed her hair back out of her face impatiently. "But that was there and now I'm here, and it's over. Period."

Jody pulled to a stop at the parking kiosk. "So, what, you're never going to date again because you made a mistake with Bennett?"

"I'm not going to get swept off my feet, again, that's for sure. I might start dating a nice man at some point," Taylor said consideringly. "Someone who's easygoing and understands what's important to me."

Jody pushed a bill at the parking attendant. "You mean a man you can twist around your little finger."

"Are you saying I've got control issues?"

"I'm saying you're so scared of being controlled that you're going to ridiculous lengths to avoid it, to the point that you're walking away from something that obviously has chemistry for no good reason.'' She took back her change and put her car in gear. ''Don't be afraid to live again, or to make mistakes. That's what life's all about.'' She punched the accelerator and headed out toward the highway.

8

THE HALLWAY THAT LED FROM the parking garage into the building was starkly utilitarian, the harsh fluorescent lighting showing each scrape and blemish on the industrial-gray walls. Walls that emanated winter chill. Even her thick funnel neck sweater and suede skirt didn't block it. She was definitely back home, Taylor thought with a sigh.

At least she was coming back to a fully refurbished office. New carpet, the landlord had promised her. Fresh paint, a new door or two, and they'd replace the discolored lighting fixtures. Anticipation buzzed through her. A person ought to come back from vacation to at least some good news.

Her shoes made a slapping noise on the tile as she reached the back door of DeWitt Travel. Frowning down, Taylor saw a small pool of water. A small plop disturbed the surface. Slowly, she looked up to see the warped and discolored panels in the acoustical ceiling. Another drop of water fell as she watched.

It couldn't be anything in her offices, she told herself as she sorted through her key ring to open the door. There was no reason to worry. It took her two tries to get the key into the lock.

Instead of the cush of new carpet, her high-heeled leather boots struck bare concrete floor in the short hall that led to the agency. Ahead of her spread an empty room. The desks were gone, the chairs were gone, the reception credenza was gone. She stifled a cry. It was as though someone had come in and gutted her office overnight, right down to the ground.

Oh, but it wasn't just the furniture that was missing from the main room, she saw as she walked through the open space, fury making a little buzz in her ears. In one corner, the Sheetrock had been torn away to expose the studs and girders. Piles of watersoaked drywall sat on the concrete. The ceiling tiles were swollen or broken loose and wires dangled from holes where the new light fixtures were to go in. Rolls of carpet and padding lay against one wall.

Eyes wide, she whirled to look behind her, where her personal office and the combination lunch room/ mail room formed the back of the office. Both were crammed with the missing furniture. The new carpeting, a handsome royal-blue, was already laid in those rooms but not in the main space.

The main space that was due to be open for business in half an hour.

"What the hell?" asked a familiar voice.

Taylor looked up to see Nicole, her senior agent, standing at the front door. "I take it you don't know anything about this?" Taylor asked.

"I worked out of my apartment the whole time you were gone. I thought they were supposed to be done by today."

"They were."

"Well, what happened?"

"That's exactly what I intend to find out," Taylor said grimly. She headed toward the door just as a pair of jacketed workmen walked in carrying tools.

"Hey, you're not supposed to be in here," said

one. Burly and ruddy-faced, he held a prybar and looked at her suspiciously.

"This is my business," she returned. "I'm supposed to be working here right now. What happened?"

He shook his head. "Pipe got broken is what I heard. You'll have to check with the boss. The water soaked all the Sheetrock, messed up the carpet." His partner began ripping out the crumbling wall panels. "We're supposed to put up new drywall today."

"How long's that going to take?"

"Lady, I don't know. Ask the prime, it's his headache. Our job is just to get the new drywall hung and mudded and then it's somebody else's problem."

"You'd better believe it's somebody else's problem," Taylor said grimly. "This was supposed to be done last week."

"I don't know nothing about that," the burly workman allowed. "You oughtta check with the boss. He's in the trailer outside." He fingered his prybar. "We'll get it done as quick as we can."

Taylor knew where the trailer was. A weathered tan, it sat on a side street abutting the building. She whirled and marched out the door, her heels ringing on the concrete floor.

"What are you going to do?" Nicole asked from behind her.

"Stay here," she snapped. "I'm going to find out what the hell is going on."

Taylor's mental temperature had raised to full boil by the time she hit the pedestrian tunnel. Her landlord had been very clear about the dates her business would need to be closed in order to allow renovations in her space and to the facade of the building. The closure had been the reason she'd given herself the luxury of a vacation, her first in years. She'd been expecting to return to a whole new look for the place.

It was a whole new look all right. A look of disaster. She'd been out of her mind to sit down in Mexico and trust people to do their jobs, she railed at herself. She knew better than that. Leave nothing to chance, it was the first rule of business ownership.

Still, that was no excuse for the contractors. This whole mess was completely unprofessional. They were supposed to get it done, plain and simple. That was their job. They had a schedule, she had a business. She wasn't about to be bankrupted by their incompetence.

Taylor stopped at the trailer steps, not even trying to cool the fury that boiled in her blood. Sometimes, calm was the best way to get things done, but sometimes letting loose made more of an impression. Slapping a hand on the door latch, she wrenched it open, and mounted the steps to walk into the trailer.

And found herself face-to-face with Dev Carson.

THERE WERE TIMES, DEV THOUGHT, when the whole world seemed to stop for just an instant. Times like this. High color stained her cheekbones, her eyes were stunned, it was the face that had haunted his dreams since she'd left him in Mexico. He'd thought of her throughout the interminable hours of his trip home, the scent of her lingering in his mind, the feel of her skin a memory in his fingertips. For a vacation fling, she'd carved herself quite a spot in his head.

He didn't give a damn what he'd agreed to, he wanted more.

Gone was the bronze sarong, the turquoise bikini,

the hot pink sundress. The woman who stood before him now was an urban sophisticate in expensive boots and a forest-green wool coat. Her smoothly coiffed hair was a far cry from the sun-streaked, finger-combed tangle it had been the week before.

That wasn't the only thing that was different. The lazy indolence was gone. Tension vibrated through her, and he was pretty certain it was aimed at him.

"What the hell are you doing here?"

He'd expected anger, but she seemed more shaken as she found her voice.

"I work here."

"You what?"

He could see the instant it sank home and the shock morphed into fury. He'd expected her to be angry. The intensity, though, surprised him. "I work here. My partner and I are the prime contractors."

"You mean you've been here all along?"

"How do you think I found your agency?" he asked reasonably.

She narrowed her eyes. "Why didn't I ever see you?"

He shrugged, staring at the fragile line of her neck, wondering if she still wore the same scent. "My partner and I have a couple of projects going. I was mostly working over at the Peabody renovation until I had a good reason to be here."

"Why didn't you tell me?"

He couldn't resist baiting her. "You never asked."

"Don't give me that. We agreed that things were supposed to be over after we got home."

"So? I didn't figure any job played into our agreement."

"You work practically in my front yard and you

don't think it plays into ending the affair once we get home?''

''You had to know I lived here somewhere,'' he said reasonably. ''We agreed, not to track each other down after we came home, and I didn't, did I? I'm just here working.'' He leaned a hip on his desk. ''In fact, right now I'd say you're the one who's coming after me.''

She smiled grimly. ''You think I'm coming after you now, buddy, you just wait. My goddamned office is a wreck.'' She stalked toward him and he felt his own temper stir.

Taylor wasn't the only one who was good and ticked off. The sun-soaked relaxation of Mexico was a fast disappearing memory. He'd come back to chaos, delays, and a boatload of excuses from the subcontractors, with a partner who was nowhere in sight. ''They ran into some problems while I was gone,'' he said.

''And you never thought about coming home early to deal with them, did you? I guess lying around on the beach was a bigger priority.''

He'd known nothing about it, though it wasn't any of her business. ''Did you call your office when you were in Mexico?''

''What's that got to do with anything?''

''Did you?''

She held on to the thin thread of temper. ''No, I didn't call my office.''

''Neither did I,'' he said shortly. ''As I recall, neither of us had much time for that.''

She flushed even as her eyes darkened. ''Don't go there, Carson, not if you value your health.''

He ran a finger down her cheek, smiling when she

jerked her head away angrily. "Why, you going to hurt me?"

"Don't get cute. I've got a business to run. I can't afford to stay closed another couple of weeks while you get your act in gear." She stepped forward and got in his face. "I've got no flooring, no lights, no power," she said, stabbing him with a forefinger to punctuate her words. "In some places I don't even have a goddamned ceiling or walls. My unit was supposed to be finished last Friday. You want to explain to me what the hell is going on and why I'm not ready to open up in half an hour?"

"Careful, darlin'," he said softly, anger mixing with arousal in him.

"No, you be careful," she retorted heedlessly. "I want my office put together enough to work. I want furniture out where I can get to it, and I want power."

"We've got to get that whole section of the building rewired before we can get you turned on."

"I want you to get me turned on by tomorrow."

His control snapped and he reached out to sweep her toward him. "How about right now, instead?" He heard her surprised intake of breath before he pulled them both into the kiss, into the familiar cocoon of hot darkness.

He'd thought she was sexy when she was relaxed on the beach. She was hotter still, with her eyes flashing and her cheeks stained with color. And it was unbearably tantalizing to feel her body tense and her arms push against him even as her mouth softened and began to kiss him back.

Suddenly he found himself swept into a torrent of sensation that was swifter and rising faster than he'd guessed. It was as though his footing was disappearing and he was clutching on to her to anchor himself, to anchor them both. He'd intended to show her she wasn't immune, he'd thought to ease some of the ache for her that throbbed through him, but he never expected it to sweep him past all of that and into an insatiable hunger.

Taylor broke the kiss, breathing hard, eyes dark. "Keep away from me," she said shakily. "This isn't about fun and games anymore, Carson. This is real."

"I thought last week was pretty real." He kept his grip on her upper arms.

"No. Last week was fantasyland, and it's over. I don't need you grabbing me and kissing me and I don't want it."

There she was again, flinging out challenges. "Funny, I could have sworn you were kissing me back." He concentrated on leveling out his own system.

Her gaze iced over him even as she rested her hands on his chest. "I don't care if we boffed our brains out in Mexico all last week, it doesn't mean anything now. I want to know your plan to fix my unit, Carson, or I go to the landlord."

With a clunk, the door swung open. Taylor and Dev jerked apart as a redhead with a boyish looking face stepped into the trailer. He could have been a teenager still, but for the faint beginnings of lines around his gray eyes.

"Sorry to interrupt." His eyes flicked back and forth between Taylor and Dev as though he were unsure of what to do next. Finally he settled on Dev. "I thought you might be back today," he said, just a hair too pleasantly.

"I thought you might be showing up for work," Dev said, with a glance at his watch.

"I had car trouble." His grin faltered. Dev stared at him impassively.

"That's nothing compared to what you've got now. Taylor DeWitt, this is Riley Caldwell, my partner. Taylor runs the travel agency on the ground floor."

"Sure." Riley's eyes flicked to Dev even as he took Taylor's hand. "Sorry for the problems we've had in your unit."

"I appreciate that, but it's not much of a help," Taylor said flatly. "I'm more interested in what you and your partner can do to speed up the repair process. I'm losing money every day my office is closed."

"Look, Riley and I need to talk scheduling," said Dev. "Why don't you go get yourself some coffee and we'll crunch some numbers. I'll get you a revised timeline in about fifteen minutes."

"It better be good, Carson, that's all I've got to say." She turned around and walked out.

Riley walked over to the door and checked the latch. "So what was that all about?"

"You mean why's she ticked off? You heard."

"Not enough, apparently." Riley tapped the wall lightly with his knuckles. "These walls are kind of thin, you know. It sounded like the end of a real interesting chat."

"Which is beside the point right now," Dev said steadily.

"I mean, if you're going to start bringing women in here," Riley began.

Dev cut him off. "The only women who are coming in here are the ones whose offices have been flooded. You want to tell me what the hell happened with her unit? It was supposed to be done last week.''

Riley scratched his neck. "It was done, at least mostly."

"Look, you said you could keep track of this job and the renovations at the Peabody while I was gone. You said we didn't need to hire a fill in."

Riley shifted uncomfortably. "I just had some personnel problems, and the city inspector at the Peabody got ticked when he tripped on a board and he slapped us with a whole bunch of unnecessary violations."

Dev leveled a gaze at him. "How many times have I told you to get the job site clean enough to eat on before the inspectors show?"

"Cleanliness isn't on the inspection sheet. The work was done," Riley insisted stubbornly.

Dev sighed. Over the years, he and Riley had developed a division of labor that worked. One of the key parts was having Dev manage the city inspectors and the disputes between workers. He should have known if trouble was going to crop up while he was gone, it would be rooted in those areas. "We'll take care of it. Now tell me what happened in the front unit."

"Oh, that." Riley shook his head. "They wanted another door cut into a conference room upstairs. The kid on the crew went at the wall with a saber saw. Cut clean through the inch and a half water line."

Dev closed his eyes. "Niagara on the Inner Harbor."

"Pretty much. It poured down into the lobby and into the travel agency's unit. The lobby was okay because it's mostly terrazzo and marble faced, but the agency…'' He raised his palms. ''Then again, you two might be close enough that she's not going to mind.''

Dev bristled. ''Don't.''

''I mean, even though you did just break off your engagement and all,'' Riley continued, ignoring him.

Dev folded his arms and gave Riley a dangerous stare. ''You want to tell me what this is all about? And Riley, be careful,'' he suggested.

Riley sighed and dropped into a chair. ''Melissa's been calling here for you every day since you left.''

''Good for her.'' Dev turned around and picked a coffee mug from his desk, squinting at the residue in the bottom.

''She wants to talk to you, Dev.''

''Not going to happen, Riley.'' Dev poured himself some coffee from the pot, reasoning that the hot brew would kill anything living in the cup.

Riley massaged the bridge of his nose. ''She's my cousin, Dev. You guys wouldn't have met if it weren't for me, which is something she reminds me of every single time she calls.''

''Riley, it's not your problem, okay? You're not part of it. You can tell her that for me.''

''Uh-uh.'' Riley folded his arms across his chest. ''I'm not going to tell her anything. You've got something to tell her, you do it.''

''I already told her everything I had to say when I walked in on her with that punk that your sister brought to the Jack and Jill party.''

The silence stretched out. Riley sighed. ''Yeah, I know. It was a bad scene, Dev. I'm sorry.''

''Yeah, well don't be. We weren't right for each

other and I should have figured that out a long time ago. Melissa figured it out first, that's all.''

"Yeah, well, I guess she's changed her mind.''

"I don't want to hear it," Dev said abruptly. "End of conversation. Let's talk about something more pleasant, like how much the delays from this plumbing fiasco are going to cost us.''

TAYLOR STRODE DOWN THE sidewalk, her mind roiling. He'd known. He worked practically in her lap, and the whole time they were in Mexico, he'd known it. The whole time they'd talked about an affair that was outside of real life, about cutting things off once they left, he'd known they were going to come home and be face-to-face.

She concentrated on the anger and tried to ignore the little buzz of awareness his kiss had raised. In Mexico, she'd left herself open to it, but that couldn't happen here. In the real world, she couldn't afford to take a chance like that.

Nicole sat on the bench in front of the agency, talking with Allie, Glynnis, and the other agents. They all looked up as Taylor approached.

"So what's going on?" Nicole asked.

Taylor bit down on her fury, tamping it down into professionalism. "I'm still waiting to find out. A pipe above us broke, which is what wrecked the walls and the ceiling. I don't know if it wrecked the carpet, too, or if they never got around to putting it in.''

"Wow, how long will that take to fix?" Glynnis asked.

"I'm supposed to be getting their revised schedule any minute now. Can you keep working out of your homes? We get enough e-business that it should keep you busy. This won't take long, hopefully.''

"What about me?" asked Allie.

"We'll work something out," Taylor said. "For now, you guys go home, Nicole, let's go over and get some coffee.''

As much as she hated to follow Dev's suggestion, it made more sense than standing out in the frigid air. By the time they'd gotten coffee and muffins and talked over where the business stood, Taylor was feeling calmer.

"We should be able to keep enough coming in from the e-business to keep our heads above water for another week, then,'' she said. "The corporate accounts help." Then Taylor swore.

"What?''

"The meeting with Pace-Miller. I'm supposed to have a briefing with them Wednesday.''

"Better reschedule for their facility.''

"That's where it was supposed to be anyway, but how am I supposed to put the presentation and briefing packets together?''

"I'd say you're going to take a trip to Kinko's, boss.''

Taylor gritted her teeth. "I've got a printer and a copier in the office, even though I can't get to them. If I have to pay a fortune to Kinko's for printing and copies, it's not going to come out of my pocket.'' Taylor rose. "Let's go find out what he has to say about the revised timeline.''

"He who?" Nicole asked, following her.

She paused. "The contractor," she said shortly. The man who was off-limits to her in any way, shape, or form. She couldn't afford it, she reminded herself, she quite simply could not do it. Mexico had been fun, it had been…well, extraordinary, if she was honest, but that had been because it was a fling that had no bearing on their real lives.

"Hey," Nicole said as they emerged from the pedestrian tunnel at the entrance to the agency. "Isn't he that guy that got all mad about his insurance?"

Taylor nodded. "There's a reason he came to us, apparently. He was in the neighborhood."

"God, he's even better looking now than he was before," Nicole breathed.

In fact, Dev looked tough and capable, and enormously sexy. It was only Pavlovian conditioning, Taylor thought, that stirred up low level arousal just at the sight of him. For a week, seeing him had meant sex. Conditioning. That was all it was.

"Try to concentrate on business," Taylor said, as much to herself as to Nicole. "That pretty face could put us all out of a job if he doesn't get his act together."

They came to a stop in front of Dev. "Nicole Stanley, Dev Carson. Nicole's my senior agent. So what have you figured out about the office?"

"We're going to be doing everything we can to get it in working condition as soon as possible."

"And what does that mean?"

Dev consulted his clipboard. "I've got my foreman checking status in here, but it looks like the leak upstairs is fixed. The electricians are going to finish up the rewiring in a couple of hours." He walked through the glass door of the agency, Taylor trailing him.

Extension cords snaked through the door from a generator a few doors down. The growl of drills came from the far end of the room, where the crew was already replacing missing panels of Sheetrock. The swollen, discarded panels sat in a pile on the concrete floor. Taylor tasted grit in the air.

"Peter," Dev called.

A Nordic-featured blonde looked up and set aside the drill he held, walking over to Dev. "Hey, boss, what's up?" he asked, nodding at Taylor and Nicole.

"I need a status report," Dev returned.

Peter smiled at Nicole, then focused on Dev. "Sorry. They've got maybe another three hours to get the rock hung, then we need to mud it. I'll be keeping an eye on things here for a while. They'll probably be finished by the end of the day. We'll need to have the heaters in overnight. When are we going to have the power up in here?"

"I just checked with Ron," Dev said. "He's saying early afternoon we should be live."

Peter nodded. "If we have the heaters up overnight, then the Sheetrock guys can do the second coat of mud tomorrow and finish on Wednesday. One more day for sanding and we should be all set. Call it Friday for good measure," he finished.

"That's the soonest you can do?" Taylor asked.

"Some things you can't rush," he said equably.

Dev nodded. "Stay on them, Peter."

"He can stay on me anytime," Nicole muttered into Taylor's ear.

"Down, girl," Taylor said over her shoulder, then turned back to Dev. "So what's the story?"

He was scratching numbers on his clipboard, then he looked up. "You heard Peter. For the Sheetrock alone, we're looking at four days minimum, not counting painting."

"Not good enough, Carson, try again."

"Look, the plaster that covers the seams has to dry before we can sand it. There's no way to hurry it, it's not a matter of working nights or something."

"But we ought to be able to come in and use the front part of the room now, right?"

"You want to work with banging in the background and plaster dust sifting into your hair?"

"If you could get some of the furniture out of my office, I could work in there. The other agents are going home. It's just me. I can shut the door."

"You could if you had one," he said mildly.

"Look, I have a presentation I have to get done, and to do that, I need my workspace," she told him, desperation vying with irritation for control of her voice. "Hang plastic from the ceiling if you have to, I don't care, but I need to be in here."

"You're going to need to ditch the fancy clothes and wear jeans." He studied her and then nodded slowly. "All right, if you don't mind the concrete, we can get you in today. We'll curtain off the area and get your office clear. Does early afternoon sound okay?"

She nodded.

"We'll bring out the reception credenza and a desk or two."

"If you can just clear out my office and the mail room so I can get in there to work, I'll be fine."

Dev nodded. "The guys can finish hanging the rock and mudding while you're here. We can do the flooring and wire the fixtures at night. It won't be pretty, but you'll be in business, assuming you don't mind us being in and out of here."

"As long as we're open, and it doesn't last forever, I don't care."

"Then take a break and come back at one-thirty. We'll get the furniture out. You'll be ready to go by afternoon."

Taylor turned to Nicole. "Why don't you take the rest of the day and work at home? No reason you should wait around."

"What about you?" Nicole protested.

"I want to be here to make sure it gets done."

"It'll get done," Dev said mildly.

"Yeah, that's what the landlord said when I left for the Caribbean."

SHE WAS MUCH TOO RESTLESS to sit, Taylor thought. The brisk air blowing off the Inner Harbor had her heading away from the waterfront. It felt good to walk. Maybe if she walked far enough, she could figure out what to do about Dev Carson. How the hell was she supposed to look at him, talk with him without remembering the past week? How was she supposed to talk with him without wanting to feel his skin under her hands? It had become habit, addiction, fixation.

She shivered as she thought of the feel of him sliding inside her, the warmth of his body against hers. It was a little unsettling, how quickly they'd fallen into the rhythm of laughing, of touching, of being together. It had been eerily perfect, almost as though they were lovers reunited rather than newly discovering each other.

It was the withdrawal pangs that worried her the most, though. Waking up that morning without the sleepy weight of him against her, without the warmth of his hand curved over her waist had left her depressed and discouraged. Instead of being happy to plunge back into her life, she'd found herself fighting to stay in dreamland, vaguely hoping she'd awake with Dev.

She shook her head to ward off the thought. If she'd learned anything from her disastrous marriage, it had been to beware of the romancers, of the charmers, of the ones she thought she couldn't live without. They were the ones who were disastrous to live with. Like Dev, who in such a short time had insinuated himself into her days. Now, he was threatening to unleash chaos in the professional life she'd worked long and hard to build.

But worse, far worse, was the chaos he'd unleashed in her head.

9

"HAVING A CORPORATE CLIENT relationship with DeWitt Travel not only saves you money but time." Taylor was into her pitch and rolling smoothly. She felt confident in a power suit the color of goldenrod and a cream silk blouse, using her laser pointer to detail the flashy briefing chart that she'd been working on until midnight the night before. "Your dedicated agent will have detailed information on each of your travelers. You'll get itemized group billing that will show the price paid versus lowest available. We can offer you discounts with the hotel chains listed. Our arrangements with them allow us to offer special packages any time you're flying your remote reps or clients into town for meetings."

She paused, softening them up for the kicker. "Based on your corporate travel for 2002, we could have saved your company approximately $58,000 last year in airfare alone. Your briefing packet contains a summary of the terms." Taylor took a breath. "Any questions?"

The lights turned on and the office managers of Pace-Miller Enterprises that sat around the mahogany conference table looked at her with interest. The carpet underfoot was thick and plush. To her left, floor to ceiling windows gave a high-rise view of the Inner Harbor. With satellite offices scattered around the world, Pace-Miller would launch any corporate travel agency's business into the stratosphere. They'd just moved to town, and Taylor was going to get their business if it killed her.

Leonard Preston, chief financial officer, looked thoughtfully at the list of figures in front of him. "Very impressive, Ms. DeWitt. Have you ever considered a career in sales?"

Taylor grinned, relaxing imperceptibly. "You get the right property, the facts sell themselves," she said lightly.

"Yes, well, they've certainly gone a long way toward doing that today," he said. "It's a very appealing package. We need to review this, obviously, but we should be able to get back to you within the week. Thanks for taking the time to come out."

Taking the time? If they only knew what a luxury it was to be in an office that had carpets and light fixtures, Taylor thought ruefully. Out on the street, she faced the inevitable comedown. There was something electrifying about the corporate environment, playing with the big boys. As much as she enjoyed building her agency, she was fully aware that DeWitt Travel was small potatoes. Part of her yearned for a chance to test herself more, to maybe go back and get a business degree, see what kind of career she could parlay her skills into.

Another example of her flightiness, her family would no doubt say. She could hear it already. Dump your grandmother's trust fund into this pie-in-the-sky travel agency idea and then lose interest in it. Typical Taylor.

She stopped. Stick with the business, that was the thing to do. She was in a rough patch right now, but overall things were going strong. If it wasn't glamorous, at least it was profitable. Maybe in the summer, once the construction snafu had smoothed out, maybe then she could think about trying to take a night class or two, just to see how she liked it.

And maybe she could leap tall buildings with a single bound.

THE LINES OF FLIGHT NUMBERS and fares marched across the screen, showing every possible way to get from Baltimore to Chicago. Taylor keyed down her screen, bringing up itineraries. "Sorry, Sid, there's no K class availability for Friday night. I can get you a seat, but you won't be able to upgrade."

"This is my sixth trip to the coast in the past two months. I can't take cattle car or I'll go ballistic. Taylor, honey, if you love me, get me an upgradable fare. I'll come over and kiss you," he wheedled.

"That's what I'm afraid of."

"I keep telling you, I'm a hot ticket."

"I'll tell your wife that when she calls to confirm your vacation reservations," she said, tucking her tongue in her cheek. As part of the business development team for a local Internet company, Sid Hayes spent as much time on the road as off. Over the past two years, their phone relationship had veered from straight business to friendly banter.

"Tattling to my wife? You don't play fair, DeWitt."

"I'm not worthy, Sid." She clicked the keys some more. "I can get you upgraded on the Salt Lake City to San Jose section of your trip, but not Baltimore to Salt Lake. Let me check something, though." On a hunch, she changed the itinerary and was rewarded with a hit. "How do you feel about flying out of Washington?"

"That could work. Feed me some numbers."

She'd just started to call up flights, fingers sending the keys clacking, when she heard the front door open. Since everyone in the front office was supposed to be gone, she craned her head to look out her door.

Dev Carson walked down the center of the room carrying a cylindrical heater. Something skittered around in her stomach. There was no reason a man should look so outrageously sexy in dusty jeans and a faded flannel shirt over a once-white T-shirt, but he managed it. His hair was no better combed than it had been in Mexico. His chin was dark with stubble. A worn leather tool belt hung low on his lean hips, like a gunfighter's pistol belt.

He wasn't her type, she told herself. She liked classy, sophisticated men in suits who went to the ballet. Dev Carson was off the radar.

But still, her mouth watered. Pavlov's dog, she thought, just Pavlov's dog.

There was a squawk out of the receiver where she'd let it fall away from her ear and she jumped. "Sorry, Sid. Okay, we've got you out of Washington at the same time, upgradable all the way across. Want to walk through it?" Dev ferried in two more heaters while she gave Sid flight numbers and arrival times. "We got you the hotel discount, by the way. You'll receive it on check-in."

Dev walked up and stood by her desk a moment, then leaned against it to stare down at her as she worked. The cuffs of his shirt were folded back to show strong, sinewy forearms. It made her think of watching his hands on the tiller of the catamaran. It made her recall the feel of his hands on her skin. Abruptly, as vividly as though it were happening, she remembered lying on her back, his mouth driving her up, his hands on her breasts as she clutched those hard forearms.

"Hello. DeWitt, you still there?"

Taylor cleared her throat. "Sure, a rental car is no problem." She tapped at her keyboard, navigating the software. "Okay, I'm e-mailing you the itinerary with rental car and hotel right now. Let me know if you need anything else."

"I'll be right over with that kiss."

"Great, I'll give your wife a call and get her over here to watch."

Dev looked over with a raised eyebrow.

"You're merciless, DeWitt," Sid said.

"I try."

She hung up and turned to Dev.

He studied her, his eyes that cool, drift-glass green. "You sound like quite the pro."

"I have my moments. What are you doing here?" Direct was the best tack, she decided. The thing was to focus on business, not on the feelings rippling through her. He was a vulnerability she couldn't afford to have, a risk she couldn't afford to take. It was that simple.

"I need to do some detail work and set up heaters to dry the mud on the Sheetrock. When are you heading out?" he asked casually.

Now, she wanted to reply, but she had work that had to get done. More to the point, she had too much self-respect to flee. They were both adults. She could handle him. If she wasn't interested, she wasn't interested, it was that simple. "I've got a couple of hours work to catch up on."

"You sure? It's going to get pretty hot in here with three heaters going," he said, eyeing her suit.

"Can't you wait to turn them on after we leave?"

He shook his head and lit one heater, then the next, then the next. "They're butane. Open flames. They need to be watched or else we'll have bigger problems than drying mud."

"If you've got to run them, then run them." She shrugged. "I don't mind the heat." Even as she said it, a breath of warmth brushed over her. She was surprised at how quickly the butane heaters worked. It had to be the heaters, she told herself.

"Feel free to take off anything you need to," he said, his eyes lingering on hers. "No reason to be shy around me."

"I'm fine."

"That you are," he said, and walked off.

Automatically her head turned to follow him. She cursed herself mentally for watching, but those lanky legs in faded denim were too good to miss. Pavlov's dog, she thought.

"Nice suit, by the way." He called back over his shoulder. "Looks almost as good as your bikini did."

She wouldn't give him the satisfaction of a response, she told herself. Instead she opened her bookkeeping program. Corporate billing hadn't been done since she'd left for the Caribbean several weeks before. If she was going to stay in business, she needed revenues coming in pronto.

Out in the main office came the sound of a drill and noises of a hammer on wood. He hadn't bothered to tell her what he was working on, of course. He probably thought she was the type who would come looking for him, just to watch the flex of the muscles in his forearms, the play of back and shoulder under his shirt. He probably thought she'd still be hung up on his body, on his pretty face.

He didn't know her at all, she thought, rising to take a stack of invoices into the mail room.

One thing he did know was the heating ability of the butane heaters. With three of them aimed at the wall just next to her office, the air was rapidly approaching stifling. Taylor unbuttoned her jacket and hung it over her chair before she left the office.

She didn't precisely look for him on the brief trip to the mail room next door. After all, it wasn't as though she cared what he was up to, so long as he didn't bother her. It wasn't like she was trying to catch a glimpse of him bent over to measure the molding around a door, his ass framed in those faded jeans. In fact, she didn't care if he was around at all.

Her office, when she returned to it with a bottle of water from the refrigerator, was hotter than ever. Kicking off her shoes helped; slipping out of her panty hose and slip was even better. The printer hummed, spitting out another invoice. Despite the drop in walk-in business since the start of construction, she actually wasn't doing all that bad, she thought with some relief. The corporate income was keeping her above water. And if she loathed the hour or two that it took to update her records and print all the bills, she knew it was critical.

As the Pace-Miller deal was critical. If she landed that one, she was golden. She threw a few hypothetical numbers into her spreadsheet and beamed at the results. And it wouldn't be just general travel that she'd be working on. The Pace-Miller CFO had already asked that she set up their national sales meeting for late spring. Somewhere warm, he'd said, content to leave the details to her. Somewhere they could have the meetings in the afternoons and evenings and leave the attendees free to explore during the day, a way to make them feel cosseted while still getting work out of them. Grand Bahama, she mused, or maybe the Cayman Islands. Somewhere with hot sun and golden sand and water the color of palest turquoise.

Before she could stop it, her mind slid back to warm sun and whispering waves, to the periwinkle sky and the fantasy tracery of the coral reefs. If she closed her eyes, she could put herself back there, lying on her sun couch, feeling the heat of the sun soaking into her skin. Feeling hard, work-callused hands rubbing sunscreen into her back. Feeling those rough hands on her breasts while he drove into her from be—

"If you closed your eyes, you could pretend we're back in Mexico." The words had her jumping in her seat. Dev stood in her doorway, his flannel shirt gone, the short sleeves of his T-shirt showing off the hard curves of his biceps. "Sorry, didn't mean to startle you."

The flush crept up her cheeks. "I was…I was just taking a break."

Dev glanced over at the panty hose and slip tossed on her guest chair and raised his eyebrows. "Must have been some break."

Now she was blushing furiously, he noticed. "Did you want something?" she asked, an edge to her voice.

You, naked, on top of me. "I just wanted to let you know I'm installing the molding around your doorway here."

"Be still my beating heart. Am I actually going to get a door next?"

"Good things come to those who wait." Good things like making love with her, though he didn't think he'd find it very easy to wait for that. Not when he was looking at the soft vee of skin where the neckline of her blouse fell open, while the sheen on her skin reminded him of the way she'd looked after they'd just tumbled out of bed.

"Am I going to have to wait long to have a door?"

"I'll probably get to it in the next night or two. In the meantime, you'll be a model boss, have the ultimate open door policy."

"You have to actually *have* a door to have an open door policy," she said dryly.

"Look at this as practice."

She snorted and turned back to her spreadsheet, absently fanning herself with a folded piece of paper. Dev ran the measuring tape up one side of the doorway, writing the measurement on the unfinished paper of the Sheetrock, where it would be painted over later. Because he was meticulous and left little to chance, he measured the other side of the doorway as well. To some contractors, a molding that ended an eighth of an inch above the floor was no big deal, especially in an office. To him, it was a matter of being a craftsman, of building the same way he'd build for himself.

He cut the strips of metal molding to size, carrying them back over to the doorway to install them. The job just happened to afford him the perfect angle to glance in at Taylor as she nibbled on her lip in concentration. An arc of hair curved down onto her cheek and she brushed it back absently as she stared at her computer screen.

This was a completely different person than the languid, wanton he'd been with the week before. Why was it that she only fascinated him more? In Mexico, he'd glimpsed a woman who was an intriguing mix of contradictions, part free spirit, part cautious soul, with occasional flashes of vulnerability. None of it fit with the no-nonsense professional sitting in the office in front of him, yet he found himself wanting her more than ever.

The plan had been simple—get it out of their systems in Mexico, go at it like minks. Have fun and games until playtime was done.

Only he wasn't done with playtime. Every day since he'd met her, he'd woken up wanting her. Every day since he'd come back from Mexico, he'd woken alone. Watching her now had need tugging at him. Need, and a quiet certainty that they were far from finished with each other.

PERIPHERAL VISION WAS A curse, Taylor told herself. You couldn't see enough for it to be useful, yet there it was, a distraction. All she wanted to do was finish her billing, she thought, staring at her computer screen, but focusing on the sweep of motion in her peripheral vision included Dev. Too much Dev for her to concentrate.

Even after he finished working on her doorway, she found herself straining to hear his movements, wondering what he was doing. When her mind wandered for the hundredth time, Taylor finally gave up and shut down her computer. The last thing she needed was to make a mistake on a corporate account.

Shaking her head, she covered her computer and gathered up her things. Nope, it was time to go home. At least then she could concentrate on something besides the muscles in Dev Carson's arms. *Who do you think you're kidding?* She sighed. Okay, so whether she was in the office or at home, she'd still be focused on him. That much was a given, but it didn't have to mean anything. Of course she was thinking of him. He was the first man she'd slept with in five years and now he was working practically in her lap. It was only natural that he'd be on her mind for a day or two.

She grabbed the tarp to pull it over her desk and a snow flurry of plaster dust rose into the air and settled over her, making her sneeze. Lovely. Just what her best suit needed, she thought, brushing it off in irritation. She turned to the coat rack in the corner to grab her purse and overcoat. She could use another dry-cleaning bill like she could use a hole in the head.

What a relief it would be to have the construction over with. No more mess, no more chaos, no more noise at inopportune moments.

No more Dev.

Key in hand, she walked up to the front of the room, skirting the receptionist's credenza, only to find Dev on his knees in front of the door, pressing gray slate squares down onto putty. He looked up inquiringly at the sound of her heels.

"I just wanted you to know I'm leaving. Can you lock up?"

He concentrated on setting the last tile, then stirred his bucket of putty. "You can't go out this door."

"I sort of figured that out. I leave through the parking garage anyway."

Dev looked out the front glass at the darkness. "I'm done here. Give me five minutes to close things up and I can walk you out."

"You don't need to, thanks. I'll be fine."

"You're in downtown and it's dark. Why take the chance?"

The chance she'd be taking was spending any more time with him than she had to. "I don't want to hold you up. You're already working late."

He cursed mildly and rose to his feet. "It'll take five minutes."

"I can walk myself out."

Something flickered in his eyes. "You start to walk out of here and I'll come after you and throw you over my shoulder," he said evenly. "There's absolutely no reason for you to take a risk. Now *sit!*"

Fuming, Taylor sat. As much as she hated to admit it, he was probably right. The parking garage exit had always creeped her out. She wasn't leaping to step out into it alone this late at night. Of course, stepping into it with Dev Carson was hardly any safer than stepping into it with a mugger. One threatened her wallet, the other threatened her peace of mind.

TAYLOR'S HEELS CLICKED ON the tile floor of the hallway to the parking garage, in counterpoint to the soft, metronomic thuds of Dev's work boots. The laced up leather enticed her at some very basic level, just like watching him in his tool belt, moving around with graceful purpose.

He pressed on the crash bar of a door, opening it into the dim, concrete cavern of the parking garage.

"Where's your car?"

"One floor up," she said, pointing to the elevators. When the car arrived, one of the interior lights had been smashed, leaving the car dim, with gritty glass on the floor.

He punched the number on the control panel. "Now aren't you glad you've got someone along?"

"Look, it's nice of you to want to be sure I'm safe, but I really didn't need it. Quite frankly, the less time we spend together, the better. We had an agreement, remember?"

"True. But I figured as one business person to another, we might renegotiate."

"Forget it. Especially not with you working here. If I'd known about it before, last week would never have happened."

He raised an eyebrow. "Are you sure about that? It's not like you didn't know that I lived here. Or did you think I flew in to see you based on your reputation?"

Her eyes flashed at him. "Clearly, I wasn't thinking. I definitely wasn't planning to deal with you on a daily basis when I got back."

"So I guess we should revise our agreement," he said with an easy shrug. "Maybe something a little more open-ended?"

"Dream on, Carson." The elevator door opened and she stepped out, not looking to see if he followed. "I don't need any more complications in my life."

"It doesn't have to be complicated."

"Oh, get real. Nothing between a man and a woman is uncomplicated." She came to a stop by her car, keys in hand.

"On the contrary, it can be quite simple. Want me to demonstrate?" He reached for her.

"Back off." She spun to face him, her car at her back.

"Why not?"

"Because we've got a professional involvement."

"No, we don't. You don't work for me. I don't work for you." He reached out and fingered the wool of her lapel. "Not like the way we worked last week."

He was standing close enough that she could smell that elusive scent of him, a mixture of soap and shampoo and the sharpness of exertion. She shook her head to clear it. "Last week was temporary and it's over."

"Why? You're here, I'm here. We could turn up my heater and put on our bathing suits and splash in the tub, pretend we're back in Mexico. I've got some extra sunscreen…"

"There's no point to it," she replied weakly. Almost before the words were out, her imagination painted a vivid, immediate image of several points, several hot, slippery points she'd be better off not thinking of.

Dev smiled. "But that was part of the fun, wasn't it," he asked, stepping forward until she leaned back against the side of her car, feeling the driver's window at her back. He didn't touch her, didn't lay a finger on her. He just leaned in and nuzzled just behind the point of her jaw, his lips warm against the fragile skin. "This is right where you put your perfume on," he murmured, inhaling for a moment. "I used to watch you dress in the room and all I wanted to do was breathe it in forever, the way you smelled."

His lips brushed against her earlobe, then ranged

over to her chin. Taylor stood, trembling, the cool of
the car behind her, the heat of Dev's body in front of
her.

"That's when I wanted you the most," he said,
"when you were dressing. You'd put on your clothes
and all I wanted to do was get them off you and have
you naked." His tongue traced her bottom lip. "You
remember what it was like. You remember what it
felt like in the water, when I was inside you and we
were looking back at the beach, all those people lying
in the sun with no idea what we were doing out
there."

She could see it as though it were happening, feel
it. A burst of desire rocketed through her. His teeth
teased at her upper lip and she almost dissolved from
the feel of it. And then his mouth was on hers, hard
and swift. It ripped her from the chilly Baltimore
parking garage and straight back to the heat and passion of Cozumel. She remembered this, oh, she remembered the silky soft feel of his mouth, the brush
of his tongue, his elusive taste that made her only
crave more. Half dizzy, half weak, and wholly overwhelmed, she clutched at his shoulders but merely
succeeded in pulling herself closer to him.

Arousal made her breath come fast. Her mind
groped vainly for a way to anchor herself to reality.
This didn't make sense, why, she couldn't remember.
She needed to stop, to keep from being whirled away
into the person she'd been the week before. The person who took chances. The person who would risk
disaster if only it meant more kisses like this.

Walk away, she told herself.

And pulled him closer.

He wanted, and the want tore at his control. He

needed, and the need only fed on itself. If she'd told him no, if even with her body language she'd resisted, he'd have walked away. But instead, she tangled her fingers in his hair and made a sound of hunger low in her throat. And it sent him to the edge.

He cursed the bulk of their winter clothing, ripping at his gloves to get them off so that he could touch her. The freezing air bit at his skin and he cursed. They were in a parking garage, not Cozumel, he told himself desperately, and inch by inch he dragged himself back from the madness until he could release her.

Finally he made himself step away. "You should get home," he said softly. "We can finish our business later."

Taylor raised her fingertips to her lip and blinked, slowly coming back to reality. She unlocked her car and sat in the driver's seat. "We don't have any business to finish, Carson," she said, her voice not entirely steady.

He rested a hand on the door frame and leaned down to her. "If we didn't have any business to finish, Taylor, you'd have been gone long since."

10

"OKAY, TELL ME AGAIN WHY it is that you don't want to jump this guy's bones?" Jody asked Taylor as they stood in line at the movie theater.

"Well, he lied to me, for one thing."

"Not technically," Jody objected, then transferred her attention to the box office cashier. "One, please." She rummaged in her mock Kelly bag and pulled out a bill. "He just didn't bring it up."

"That's lying by omission," Taylor said obstinately. "The same," she said to the cashier.

"Not at all." Jody opened the door for Taylor to go in ahead of her, then headed for the concession line. "You agreed that it was all about Mexico, and that life back home was off-limits. Now that you're home, it's pretty clear that he still lusts after you. And you can lie to yourself all you want, you still feel the same. I don't see what you're in such a snit about."

The concession vendor gave them a brilliant smile. "And what can I get for you today?"

Jody gave Taylor an inquiring glance. "The usual?"

"Of course."

"Two Cokes, a box of Milk Duds, and a large popcorn, no butter," Jody instructed, handing a bill to the clerk. "You know, I could be like your mother and say that if you don't lighten up you'll always be buying tickets for one.''

Taylor snorted and picked up her soda and the tub of popcorn. ''That might be someone's mom, but not mine. Mine's more likely to worry that I don't have an escort to the art museum gala.''

''Same thing.''

''Don't tell my mother that.'' They headed for their theater. ''Anyway, you're missing the point. He knew what he was doing. He knew it was a problem,'' Taylor said, feeling the annoyance afresh. ''We talked about things being over when we got home. He had to know I wouldn't go for it if he was working at my office.''

''Did you tell him he was supposed to be a mind reader?''

''Cute.'' Taylor spared her a glance. ''I had no plans to see him once we got home.'' And of course she hadn't planned on being kissed senseless, either, she thought, moistening her lips. ''And now, he's practically working in my lap.''

The auditorium was hushed and only thinly populated. They gravitated to their usual seats a dozen or so rows from the front. Popcorn crunched under their feet.

''And whose fault was that?'' Jody asked, dropping into a seat near the center. ''Did he come looking for you? You were the one who told them fix your place or else. What's he going to do, pay a crew overtime or do it himself?''

''He could have gotten someone if he'd wanted to. He's working in the office just to bug me.''

''So don't let him get to you.''

Taylor gave a grumpy twist to the cap of her water

bottle. "Oh, like that's possible. You try seeing a guy you had wild sex with and not thinking about it. I'm only human, you know."

"So what's the problem?" Jody reached over and grabbed a handful of popcorn. "Is he clueless about going down on you?"

"Oh, no. He's pretty much got it refined to an art," Taylor said, not noticing that her words came out a little dreamy.

"I don't get it, then. He's gorgeous, he's obviously still interested or he wouldn't have kissed you blind last night. And you enjoyed it, don't tell me you didn't."

"He's a good kisser," Taylor allowed. "And smells great."

"So what's your problem?"

"I just don't want…" Taylor stopped and stared at the screen, where a still screen quizzed them on the name of Paul Newman's Oscar winning performance.

"You don't want what?"

She breathed out. "I don't want to make another mistake."

Jody nodded wisely. "Another Bennett."

"Another Bennett."

"Well, I can see that that could be a risk," Jody said, and tossed a piece of popcorn into her mouth. "After all, Bennett freaked about you being in a bikini on your honeymoon. And he wouldn't have sex with you. And even when you were dating, he was pathologically jealous. This Dev guy sounds like he's just like that."

"Don't make me sound stupid."

"*I'm* not making you sound anything, sweetie pie."

Taylor made a face at her. "I just don't want to get myself in a box again."

"I know, hon." Jody squeezed her shoulder. "Hey, don't listen to me. I mean, what do I know about it? You should probably follow your instincts and keep your distance. I mean, if you have the inkling he's a jerk and a potential abuser, that should be it."

"He's not a jerk."

"The last thing you need is someone pushing you around and making you feel bad about yourself," Jody continued. "If he's a twit and only out for himself, stay away from him."

"Mexico was great," Taylor said, remembering ripping up the coast with him, the wind in her hair.

"Yeah, but Mexico wasn't reality, face it." Jody shrugged. "From what I'm hearing, he's an arrogant twit you should get the hell away from. There are plenty of other guys out there."

"He's not an—" Taylor stopped herself and gave Jody a narrow-eyed look. "What are you doing?"

"Who, me?"

"I don't see anyone else around here."

"I'm trying to be supportive," she said. "If you want to hate him, then I'll hate him for you."

"I don't—"

"You don't what?" Jody blinked at her innocently.

"Nothing," Taylor muttered. "The previews are starting."

DEV SAT AT HIS DESK, studying the construction schedule. Despite the delays, they still stood to finish the project on time if he could just get a little more done in Taylor's unit. The most time-consuming part, the drywall, was done. They still needed to finish the painting, ceiling and trim work, then get the carpeting in. If they stayed on schedule with the rest of the building, they'd be all set.

It would take, he calculated, at maximum another week to work on Taylor's unit.

Working on Taylor, now, that might take longer.

He tapped his fingers restlessly on the desk. In Mexico, the one week limit had made sense. It didn't anymore. He wasn't ready to give it up. He wasn't ready to give her up.

Of course, there was no reason why he should, provided he could talk her into it. Their arrangement had worked in Mexico. There was no reason it couldn't work in Baltimore. He thought of the way she'd responded when he'd kissed her and felt that rush of heat and tightness flow through him. Oh, no, there was absolutely no reason it couldn't be just as hot back home. He just needed to convince her.

All right, so it might take some doing. She'd left early the night before, the first time she hadn't worked late the whole week. Chance, maybe. Or maybe not. He thought about the way her mouth had softened under his, the way she'd sighed and he gave a wicked smile. She might try to avoid him, but he wasn't going to make it easy for her.

The door to the trailer opened and Riley stepped inside. "Jesus, it's cold out there," he burst out, unzipping his parka and throwing down his gloves.

Dev saved his file. "It's winter. It happens like that."

"You kidding? It's March."

"Barely."

"Practically summer in some places. Remind me again why we're not working in Florida?"

"Lack of a business license, lack of connections, not to mention the fact that we've got work lined up here for about a year and a half."

"Besides that."

Dev just looked at him. "Are we on schedule at the Peabody job or did you come over here to give me some more bad news?"

"You're just cranky about coming back from your vacation to a few little kinks."

"Not to mention a string of sixteen-hour days."

"Hey, you take a month off, what do you expect? Just think how bad you'd have felt if you'd been gone all that time and we didn't even miss you."

Dev put his tongue in his cheek. "Oh, yeah, real bad."

Riley flopped into a chair and swung around to stare at the white board that tracked the project. "So how we doing here?"

"Almost caught up. Just a few more nights and we'll be on target. Want to take a look?" Dev slid his laptop toward Riley, but he just waved it away.

"Nah, the white board works for me, as long as it's up-to-date."

"Are you ever going to join us in the twenty-first century?"

Riley shrugged. "Hey, I'm in construction, why do I need computer stuff? I know how to snap a line and swing a hammer. That's all I need."

Dev snorted and worked on his planning program. The crews were finishing up the second floor carpeting, and he had a load of concrete coming in that afternoon for the new planters out front. All he needed to do was get fresh ceiling tiles installed in Taylor's office that night and they'd be ready for doors and carpet the following week. Anyway, doing the molding would afford him another excuse to see her and do some more convincing.

Not to mention get another look at that face.

Riley sat behind his desk, pulling a set of plans from his drawer. "So you called my cousin yet?" he asked idly.

Dev let his breath out slowly and searched for patience. "No, I haven't called her. Why would I?"

"I just thought you might want to give her a chance to explain."

"I walked in on her giving a guy a blowjob at our Jack and Jill party. You want to tell me what there is to explain about that?" Dev yanked open his top drawer and searched for a pen.

"It's just that she's really upset. Are you telling me you never had a couple of drinks and did something dumb?"

Dev slammed the drawer. "Something dumb? For chrissakes, Riley, we were a week away from getting married."

Riley stared at him a moment, then nodded. "Okay, okay. I was just asking."

Dev shook his head. "Yeah, well stop asking already. It's over, okay? Let's leave it that way."

IT WAS AMAZING WHAT A difference it made to cover up the white-streaked gray of the Sheetrock, Taylor reflected, admiring the freshly painted walls of the main office. True, left to her own devices she'd have chosen something more vivid, but the manila cream was a tad more creative than industrial white, and several steps up from bare drywall. Now if they could just do something about the ceiling and the floor, the place would look like a real business.

Taylor wandered up front where late-afternoon sunlight searched its way through the scaffolding outside and into the offices. The lobby area definitely needed some more pizzazz. She might not have a choice about the inner office walls, but there had to be something she could do to add some drama up front. Something to get clients excited about going away, something to give them the travel bug. Maybe a wall mural of a tropical scene in the entrance lobby, and some beach chairs. Give people the feeling they were already on vacation. Of course, she'd have to weigh that against the image she'd send her corporate clients. Granted, most of them dealt with her by phone, but still, she'd hate to send the wrong message.

Then again, once she'd gotten them on contract, the business was steady, whereas walk-ins always needed to be wooed.

The tropical mural, she decided.

"Allie, dig out the decorator catalog for me, will you?" It might have been near the end of the day, but there was still time to look at things.

Allie reached for the bookshelf just as the switchboard bleeped. "Good afternoon, DeWitt Travel. Ms. DeWitt? One moment please. May I say who's calling?" There was a click as Allie put the caller on hold and waved to Taylor. "It's Leonard Preston from Pace-Miller."

Adrenaline spurted through her. "Keep him on hold. I'll be in my office in two minutes."

Her phone was flashing when she reached her desk.

Still, she sat and took a deep breath before picking up the handset. "Taylor DeWitt."

"Ms. DeWitt, Leonard Preston, Pace-Miller. How are you?"

"Fine, thank you. And you?"

"I'm good. We've been reviewing your proposal. That was a very effective presentation the other day, by the way. Laid it all out for us quite clearly."

"I'm glad it was helpful," she said smoothly, silently wishing that he'd get to the point.

As though he'd heard her, he cleared his throat. "Well, we've had time to talk it over and do a little comparison shopping and we've decided to try DeWitt Travel for a twelve-month period under the terms we discussed."

Exhilaration flooded through her. She wanted to laugh, she wanted to whoop, she wanted to jump for joy. Instead she maintained her calm. "Excellent news, Leonard. I think you'll find it will be a beneficial relationship."

"I'm sure of it."

The grin was making her cheeks hurt, but she couldn't stop. "As we discussed, service is effective as of right now. Do you need an additional orientation session for the administrative assistants?"

"Might not be a bad idea. We could set up a telecon for the remote offices, too."

"I'll arrange it. Just get me some dates that you think will work for your folks."

"I'll have my assistant call you."

There was a singing in her head as she hung up the phone. This was big. No, huge. She had a half-dozen corporate clients already, but none on a par with Pace-Miller. Capturing that plum brought her to a whole new level. She whooped, and jumped up from her desk to go tell the troops. More business meant more work, certainly, but work that would pay off. Who knew, if the load became big enough, maybe they'd bring on another agent. She could set up a branch of the agency that would specialize in corporate travel, she thought dreamily. After that, who knew?

LIGHT WAS STILL STREAMING out of Taylor's office that evening when Dev walked into the dimmed agency, a stack of accoustical tiles under his arm. For a moment, he simply looked across the room to the bright rectangle at the back. The fact that she was still there working well after business hours didn't surprise him. The need for her that surged through him did.

Setting down the panels quietly, he paused near the open door of her office. He could hear her on the phone, laughter in her voice.

"Time to celebrate, Jody honey. We scored big today, a giant-size corporate client. None other than Pace-Miller. Yes, that Pace-Miller. Drinks are on me, and dinner at Mama Sophia's." She paused and her voice changed. "Oh, no, I totally understand. Don't you even think of giving up a chance to get laid for drinks with me. Okay, okay, don't even think of giving up a chance at dinner with a nice guy. Yes, I think Jeff's a nice guy." There was another pause. "No worries. We can go out tomorrow or Sunday. I do have other friends, you know. Sure. All right. Don't do anything I wouldn't do." He heard the click as she hung up. "Well, hell," she said feelingly. A minute passed, then she sighed and began tapping on her computer keyboard.

All pumped up and no one to celebrate with, Dev

thought with sympathy. He counted to ten before he stepped into the doorway and knocked on the open door. "Got a minute?" *Want to go to bed and not come out until next month?*

Taylor looked up at him and blinked. "What are you doing here? It's Friday night."

He shrugged. "I want to get the job on schedule. You don't have to be here, though. If you need to leave, I can close up for you."

"No, I've got work to do myself," she said, shaking her head. "Now I know why I've never gone on vacation before."

"Sucks, don't it?" he asked cheerfully. "On the other hand, sometimes the vacation is worth it."

"Sometimes." She met his gaze, and for an instant something flickered between them.

Taylor gave her head a quick shake and looked down at her desk for a moment, then glanced back up. "Well, don't let me keep you," she said briskly.

Dev nodded reluctantly. "Guess I'll get to work."

He turned to walk away. When he glanced back, he found her watching him. She looked immediately down at her paperwork. A tide of red flowed up her cheeks.

Interesting, he thought, beginning to whistle.

TAYLOR PICKED UP A COUPLE of the sheets from her printer and rose to go to the copier in the mail room, giving the sheets a final scan as she walked.

"Careful."

She jerked to a stop with her nose about a foot from Dev's butt. He stood on a ladder just outside of her office door, hoisting an acoustical panel with a hole cut in it toward the ceiling. "Jog me when I'm slipping this hole over the sprinkler head,'' he said over his shoulder, ''and I'm liable to knock loose the little plastic doohickey that keeps it from turning on. It pops loose, we got ourselves a Cozumel style rainstorm.''

She couldn't help remembering the last one she'd been in, and she knew, without a doubt, that that was exactly what he'd intended.

''Why don't you just turn off the sprinkler system?''

''It would take too much time and I want to leave for dinner.'' He slipped the tile in place surely and efficiently, then climbed back down to the ground to look at her. ''Besides, you like to live on the edge, don't you?'' With an impudent look, he shifted the ladder over, grabbed another panel, and climbed up.

''Not when it includes my livelihood,'' Taylor said. ''Speaking of which, what's the new timeline on the construction?''

Dev tipped the panel into place. ''I thought maybe you'd like to go for the industrial look. It's very popular at galleries.''

''Nice try, Carson. It's been a week and I'm getting tired of concrete and partial ceilings.''

''Look, I'm doing my best to get this done, but the longer I stand here talking to you, the longer it's going to take.''

''I have a right to know the latest timeline.''

''Not really. Strictly speaking, the landlord is the client. He's the only one who needs to know.'' He stepped down from the ladder and looked at his watch. ''Look, I don't want to waste time talking. I'm taking a dinner break. You want to find out what's going on, come with me. Otherwise, you'll just have to wait."

"I'm not going out with you," she said.

"Fine with me," he returned, "but we're wasting time here talking and I've got my mind on some crab cakes."

"You're serious."

"Hell, yeah, I'm serious. I've been working for twelve hours now. You want to talk, you're going to have to do it on my time."

Taylor's stomach growled and she flushed.

Dev grinned. "Let's get out of here. We go get some food, I can tell you where we're at, and you can tell me about your day."

"Why would I do that?"

He looked at her. "Why not?"

11

THE PLACE WAS IN FELL'S Point, a divey little joint at the end of a line of shops. An old-fashioned neon sign stuck out over the door, the name slanting up in curling yellow letters.

"Leon's?" Taylor gave him a dubious look. "I agreed to dinner, not a drink at a bar."

"It's not a bar." Dev opened the door for her. "The food's good and it's the only place I can get in wearing work clothes. You want fancy, you're going to have to wait until I'm dressed for it."

"This isn't a date, Carson."

"Whatever you say."

Leon's wasn't a restaurant and it wasn't a bar. It was a tavern. Maybe there was no sawdust on the wide-planked floor, but the walls were rough wood, the clock was a beer sign, and bowls of peanuts dotted the well-polished bar. Shadowed bulbs snaking down from the ceiling filled the room with pools of light and shadow. Tall booths lined two walls, offering privacy and darkness. A handful of tables crowded the center. On the far side, a low riser held a microphone and drums indicating the presence of a band. No surprise there. After all, it was Friday night.

How long had it been since she'd been out on a Friday night? Certainly it had been nearly forever since she'd been out with a man, not that this partic-

ular jaunt counted. This was just about taking a break
and getting some information.

Music came from the jukebox, which leaned
heavily toward blues, old R&B, and classic rock,
judging by the selections.

"I'm surprised this place isn't more packed on a
weekend."

Dev shook his head. "This is about as busy as
Leon's ever gets. It's not hot with the chichi crowd,
just with the regulars."

"And are you a regular?"

He shrugged. "I'm not enough of a drinker to be
a regular anywhere. I come here sometimes when I
don't want to hassle with cooking. It's comfortable."

It was, Taylor realized, looking around. It didn't
have the self-consciously architectural decor of the
hot clubs or the aggressively retro kitsch of some of
the chains. It was simply a place a person could be
at ease, while away the time.

"You want to sit in a booth or at the bar?" Dev
asked. "They serve at either."

"The bar." It was safer than one of the dim, intimate booths, she decided. On stools, out in the open,
with the bartender hanging around to make conversation, it couldn't help but be safe.

Then Dev caught her hand and led her to the far
end of the room and she realized that she'd miscal-
culated. Here, in the corner where the polished wood
of the bar dog-legged back to the wall was a dim nook
just big enough for two stools. With the overhead rack
for glasses hanging above them, it felt every bit as
isolated as a booth might have. At least in a booth,
they'd have been sitting across from each other, not
side by side on bar stools, close enough to touch.

The bartender came over, a grizzled man with a dark moustache and a lived-in face that suggested nothing that happened in the tavern—or out, for that matter—would surprise him. Refreshingly taciturn, he served up their drinks with an economy of motion.

"Freddy's the best part about this place," Dev said.

"I thought maybe he was Leon."

Dev shook his head and took a drink of his Guinness. "Nope, just a guy who knows how to serve drinks without talking too much."

"You said you come here to avoid going home. I'd figure you'd want company."

"I said I come here because I can't face cooking," he corrected. "I don't mind being by myself. I think silence is kind of soothing."

She felt the same way, but it still didn't fit. "Why did you want to get married if you like living alone?"

He shrugged. "I don't think living with someone means you never get peace and space. It shouldn't, anyway."

"Do you really believe that?"

"Yeah. The key is that the person you're marrying has to believe that, too. If you can sit in silence with someone and be comfortable, then you know you've really got something."

Freddie handed them menus. The selection was more ambitious than she'd have expected, leaning more toward crab cakes and baked halibut than burgers and onion rings. She chose Yankee pot roast and hoped she wouldn't be sorry.

"So what's the update on the construction?" Taylor asked, laying down her menu.

"Not so fast." Dev raised his glass. "Tell me about your day."

She flushed. "Why?"

"Because I like listening to you talk."

"Running a travel agency isn't exactly exciting stuff," she warned.

"It means enough to you that you do it for a living."

She gave him a suspicious look. "This isn't some kind of ploy to get me into bed, is it?"

Humor flickered in his eyes. "I don't use ploys and I already know how to get you into bed."

She'd have been better at shutting him down if he hadn't made her want to laugh. "Why don't you tell me about your day, instead?"

"I spend all day talking to people. I'd like to listen for a change. What's the best thing that happened to you today?"

Taylor hesitated, then decided to take him seriously. "I got a new client."

"You mean you sold a new vacation?"

She shook her head. "No, this is a big fish. I landed a corporate client, a multinational one that just moved to Baltimore."

"Who is it?"

"Pace-Miller."

He gave a low whistle and raised his glass. "You don't mess around. How'd you land that fish?" he asked, clinking his glass against hers.

Taylor grinned. "With lots of good bait and twenty-pound test line. And it's going to stay landed, if I have anything to say about it. Pace-Miller is going to make a huge difference to my bottom line."

Dev glanced down at where she perched on her bar

stool. "Oh, I don't know, I kind of admire your bottom line as it is."

She laughed before she could remember to be ticked off.

"Congratulations," he went on. "Really, that's great news. I've got to believe that you had some serious competition."

"Probably," she allowed. "I got in early. I've been after Pace-Miller since the day I got wind of their move."

"Sounds like the construction biz. Strike early if you want to get the advantage."

"Do you like it, going after work?" she asked curiously.

He shrugged. "It's part of the job, like billing. How about you?"

"I'm with you on billing, but I kind of like recruiting clients. There's something exciting about it."

"The thrill of the chase?"

"Maybe." She reflected. "It's a challenge to see if I can do a better job building a package and pitching than the competition."

"Is that your favorite part?"

"Are we ever going to talk about the construction?" she asked, more amused than annoyed.

"Later." He dismissed it and took a beer nut out of the bowl in front of him. "Let's talk about your work."

"Why?"

"Because I'm curious." Because he'd gotten to know one person in Mexico and a completely different person in Baltimore, and it intrigued him. "What part is the most fun for you?"

"Pitching," she said without hesitation. "I like

building the package, but I really love getting up there and giving them a spiel that gets them right between the eyes.''

''Maybe you missed your calling.''

''What do you mean?''

''Maybe you're really cut out to be a boardroom barracuda,'' he said, resting one elbow on the bar.

''You've got to have an M.B.A. to do that kind of thing.''

''So go back to school.'' When Taylor snorted, he leaned toward her. ''Don't blow it off. This is your thing, your eyes light up when you talk about it.''

''What about you?''

He grinned. ''My eyes light up when I swing a hammer.''

''Seriously.''

''I am serious,'' he said, rubbing at the calluses on his palm.

''Then why are you running your own business?''

He mulled it over. ''I guess I like orchestrating the whole thing, too,'' he said slowly. ''You know, figuring out how to get people to pitch in together, making sure everything's in the right place at the right time, and working out a solution when it isn't. It's like the steps of a dance. I don't know, it's hard to explain,'' he said, glancing away.

''No, I see exactly what you mean. A job like renovating my building has got to be huge.''

''It's kept us busy, though I'm sorry about the delays.''

''Don't be.'' She hesitated. ''You've been working your behind off to make it up. I'm grateful for that.''

He raised an eyebrow. ''You've been monitoring my behind?''

Dinner arrived, saving her from replying.

Taylor laid her napkin in her lap and looked at the plate Freddy set before her. If she didn't expect too much, it was unlikely she'd be disappointed. Then she took the first bite, and closed her eyes in bliss. Oh, no, she wasn't disappointed. In fact, she was so far from disappointed that she wasn't even in the same universe. Leon's, quite simply, had a genius in the kitchen.

Conversation died off, the truest measure of a good meal. The tavern wasn't a place that demanded conversation or attention. It was, purely and simply, a place to relax and enjoy.

Dev smiled as she started to slow down. "Not what you'd expected, huh?"

"I like to think I have an open mind," she said with dignity.

"Yeah, right. I know what you thought you'd get…greasy burgers, limp fries, maybe some chicken nuggets. You ought to have more faith in me."

"I've seen the error of my ways," she said lightly, eyeing his crab cakes. "And how's your dinner?"

"Good," he said, fighting a smile at the avaricious look in her eyes. "You want to try some?" he asked, cutting a piece loose and offering it to her. "I'll trade you for some of the pot roast."

Taylor accepted the bite. Baltimore did crab cakes like no place else, she thought, then closed her eyes to better appreciate the flavor. When she opened them, she saw Dev watching her.

"I have never in my life seen a woman enjoy food the way that you do," he said. "Usually they're picking away or ordering salads because they're on a diet."

Taylor laughed. "It's a chick thing. Don't let a guy see you eat, especially a good-looking guy."

"I think you just gave me a compliment."

"Now, see, I can eat in front of you because I'm not expecting anything to happen between us," she went on conversationally, ignoring him.

"Mmm. Careful," he said slowly, studying her. "That sounds a lot like a challenge."

She swallowed, her eyes locked on his, her throat suddenly dry. He'd come up on her unawares, putting her at ease, making her think him harmless. He didn't seem harmless anymore. In the dim light, his eyes had a silver cast, the eyes of a predator who would not be dissuaded from what he wanted. And in the dim light, with his thigh hard and warm against hers, she couldn't be sure it wasn't what she wanted, too.

A startling twang of guitar strings broke into the moment, and she breathed a sigh of relief. In Mexico, an affair between them could be light and easy. Here in Baltimore, it seemed less likely.

With a few clicks of the drumsticks, the band broke into its opening number and Taylor straightened.

"This is such a great dance song," she said, tapping her fingers on the bar. "I used to *love* this when I was in college." She moved her shoulders to the beat.

Dev caught her hand. "Let's go cut a rug."

She threw a glance of disbelief at the empty dance floor. "There's no one out there."

"So?"

She shook her head. "Not my thing. Back in the day, maybe, but not now." Back in the day, she'd liked an empty floor best of all, because it gave her all the room she could want, because she knew she looked good. Because it made her the center of attention.

Now, she'd been cured of being the center of attention and she had no idea if her dance moves looked even moderately coordinated, let alone appealing. Nope, not even on a half-empty floor.

Still, her foot tapped and the music called to her.

"You know, I remember someone telling me not so long ago that they were finding their way back to someplace they'd been a long time ago."

Taylor flushed. "That just slipped out."

"The person I was with in Mexico wouldn't have balked at going out on an empty floor."

"I didn't know anybody there."

"You don't know anyone here now. Freddie is sure as hell not going to care. The only one who cares is you. So why not?" Dev caught her hand in his. "Come on out with me. Find Taylor again."

The dance floor seemed enormous. Dev led her onto it, pulling her to the center when she would have huddled on the edge by a table. She stepped from side to side, snapped her fingers, and suddenly the beat took hold of her. It was like being caught up by a wave, the way that the music seemed to move her muscles without her even trying. Motions that she'd forgotten came back. Delighted, she found herself vamping, spinning, whipping her arms to the music.

This was the person she'd once been, the person who wasn't self-conscious, who didn't care what people thought. The light feeling that had come over her in Mexico returned, a sense that she was starting to fit into her own skin again. The professional, the drudge was part of who she was, she knew that, but this was part of who she was also. It was like welcoming herself home.

The band moved straight into another song. Taylor didn't notice when more couples began to move onto the floor. She danced close to Dev, laughing into his face, galvanized by the music. When she turned too exuberantly, glancing off another dancer and bouncing against Dev, she didn't object that he put his hands on her hips to steady her.

Hot and out of breath, they grinned at each other. The music turned into a bluegrass tune with a fast beat. When Taylor would have turned away, Dev caught her hands and moved into the step. He urged her in and out, back and forth, until she got the hang of it, following the push and pull of his arms. Her feet thumped the floor to the beat. Then he started to turn her. First it was just an underarm turn, then he was reeling her in and whirling her out until she was breathless and giddy and laughing. He spun her in so they were side by side and she was cradled by his arms. As he walked them in a circle, she registered the feel of his hard body next to her and the heat of his arms around her, a little dizzy and off balance until he spun her back out.

The band wound up with a finishing flourish just as Dev pretzeled her back toward him in a double handhold. The final note hit even as she turned to grin at him.

And found his mouth too close. Awareness thudded through her. The moment seemed to stretch out interminably.

Abruptly the band shifted gears into a ballad, a slow, sexy throb of rhythm and blues. Couples moved together. Dev unwound her and started to pull her toward him.

"Dinner's getting cold," Taylor said, quickly twisting out of his arms and beating a hasty retreat back toward the bar stools.

His long legs carried him back to her more quickly than she'd expected. "For being out of practice, you did a pretty good job out there."

Taylor reached her stool and took a long pull on her beer. "It was fun. Thanks for talking me into it."

"My pleasure."

"Where did you learn to do the spinning stuff?"

He looked, of all things, embarrassed. "I lived in Savannah for a while. One of the guys I worked with had a thing for cowboy bars. You pick it up after a while."

"And then you pick the girls up," she said dryly.

Sometimes he had, though the hasty liaisons always left something of a bad taste in his mouth after. Somewhere along the line he'd just given it up, and hadn't much missed it.

Taylor, now, Taylor he'd miss.

Inside him, some thread of awareness started to thrum. The ache for her that had begun to permeate his days began to throb more insistently. The ache for the old Taylor, the chance taker. The ache for the new Taylor, the one who was as focused as he. The ache for the woman next to him, the one who'd been on his mind, interfering with his sleep, breaking his concentration ever since he'd come back from Mexico.

She gave up picking at her dinner, pushing the plate away.

"Big lunch?" Dev asked, watching her.

"No lunch at all," she said. "Bad habit of mine."

"You seemed to have more of an appetite in Mexico."

"Mexico was different," Taylor said slowly, looking down along the bar.

He reached out and touched a finger to her chin, turning her to face him.

"Why?"

"That's not who I am anymore."

He shook his head. "I don't believe that. It's not all of who you are, but it's part of you, the same part of you that was out there dancing tonight."

"I only did that because you pulled me out there."

"You wouldn't have gone if you hadn't wanted to. That person is as much a part of you as the corporate pitch artist. You just lost her for a while. Now you're getting her back."

"I should never have told you that."

Dev's eyes were dark in the shadows, his gaze focused, intent. Taylor felt like she was standing on the sand at the edge of the water, feeling it melt away under her feet in the face of the oncoming waves. She ran a hand through her hair, resting her elbow on the bar.

"Why do the two Taylors have to be separate?"

"Because it doesn't work. I can't be that person anymore." I don't have the courage, she thought.

"You've got the courage to be whoever you want to be," he said, as though he'd heard her, reaching out to take her hand in his, turning her to face him.

Heat spread through her. What she wanted, with a suddenness that nearly overwhelmed her, was him.

"Mexico doesn't have to be a place that exists outside of time and real life," he said, leaning close to her, his words soft, compelling. "I'm the same person now as I was then. And I still want you."

The words hung in the air as Taylor tried to remember how to breathe. In Mexico, it had been simple. She'd wanted and she'd taken. Now, it was no longer simple, and the need that sliced through her was far sharper.

"Come home with me," Dev whispered into her ear. "Let me take you places." His lips grazed her jaw. His fingers slid up her nape and into her hair. He nipped at her lower lip.

And heat exploded through her.

THERE WASN'T AN OLD TAYLOR, a new Taylor, a Taylor in Mexico, a Taylor at home. There was just a Taylor who wanted. Desire flowed through her veins in an intoxicating cocktail, bringing with it a lightness that made her giddy.

She pressed herself against Dev, dropping kisses on his neck as he made the short drive from the tavern to where he lived. They pulled up beside his house, a looming bulk that gave an impression of the sort of Victorian Gothic that Mr. Rochester would have lived in. No lights were on. Maybe that meant no roommates, she thought hopefully. She didn't want to share the moment with anyone, didn't want to think about anyone or anything but Dev. If it alarmed her that the ravenous need felt so right, she'd deal with it later. Having him now was vital. Whatever the next day would bring, there would be time enough to face it.

Their feet thudded hollowly on the wooden porch, and then they were inside, the front door closing behind them.

"Roommates?" she managed to say.

"No way," Dev said, pulling off her coat and dropping it on the floor.

Impatience ruled him. He had to see her, to touch her, to have her. Light and enticing, her scent wove into his senses. Another time, he'd have been patient, deliberate, seducing her over the course of an evening. Now, need blinded him, bound him to her with one single driving desire—to have her. He plundered her mouth, tasting her urgency and need, let his hands rove over her, tantalizing himself with the feel of her taut and quivering against him. In between, he whipped off his jacket, tore at the laces of his boots.

He'd known her body before, countless times. How was it that it all now felt new? When he pulled her sweater over her head, and looked at her in only her lacy demi bra, it was as though he was seeing her for the first time. When he felt her hands stroke down the muscles of his belly, the sensation had his toes curling in anticipation of what came next. Her soft sigh only made him more greedy to hear the sound of her orgasm as she clenched around him.

Taylor reached out to unbutton the fly of his jeans and pushed down, sinking to the carpeted stairs, she pulled him toward her, rubbing the tip of his hard cock against her lips. God, she'd missed this, the feel of him in her hands, his desire for her made palpable. At the sound of his groan, the sense of power surged through her. She could give him this, pleasure that made him shudder, that had his fingers twisting in her hair. The want was not hers alone, it clutched them both, dragging them closer to madness.

Dev groaned and pulled away, tugging her up against him for a hot, melting kiss. She wanted to linger, glorying over every instant. She wanted to feel him against her, in her, now. The urgency swelled, became towering, overwhelming everything else. There would be time later, she thought fleetingly. For now, she couldn't wait.

Caught up, perhaps, by the same thought, Dev broke the kiss and turned her to face the stairs.

"Up," he murmured, biting at her shoulder.

She could feel how hard he was, how ready. She knew how close she was to tumbling over the edge herself. To be taken was what she craved, taken hard so that she felt it in her every fiber. She needed to know that he was as ravenous for it as she.

"Hurry, go," he muttered, his cockhead trembling against her butt, his hands urging her upward.

"No," she countered, reaching back to pull him against her, leaning forward to stretch over the stairs. "Now."

"Now," he breathed, and she cried out as he slid up into her.

The pile of the wool stair runner was soft under her fingers. His hands were hard and urgent on her ribs, his cock was hot and urgent inside her. The sense of being plundered had her shivering with delight; when his fingers searched out the slick cleft at the front of her, she moaned. "Harder," she managed, crying out as he pounded into her until she felt him through every bit of her body.

"You want it harder?" he panted, his hands driving her, his body surging against hers.

She shivered with every stroke. He was taking her somewhere unknown, toward some edge of dark glory and delight. The days of temptation, the nights of longing, the moments of sensual extravagance had blended and intertwined to bring them to this place, to this instant, to this precipice.

And when the torment of his touch flung her over, she cried out in shock, her body bucking and jolting through the aftershocks even as he clenched her against him and groaned.

MORNING SUNLIGHT SHONE INTO Taylor's eyes, had her blinking groggily. Thank God it was Saturday, was her first coherent thought. The second was what the hell was she doing?

The night rolled back to her. Catnaps were all they had managed between the flash and the fury of their reunion. In his dimly lit bedroom, they'd relearned each other, only to discover new places and fresh needs. In the brief instants they managed to nod off, the slightest movement, the lightest brush of skin against skin, leg against leg, sent hunger rocketing through them again.

Dev lay next to her, fast asleep, his face in the pillow and one arm draped over her waist. Taylor looked around the room she hadn't even registered the night before. The house was a Victorian, that much she knew. Fluted moldings rippled around windows that had to be two yards tall. A crown molding accented the edge of the ceiling.

She could see where he'd done some work patching the walls and woodwork. More renovations, she thought with a smile, turning to roll away.

His arm tightened. "Why is it you're always trying to run away in the mornings?" he murmured, pulling her back into his arms.

"I really should check in with the office. We're open today."

"Don't your agents have keys?" he asked, brushing his hand over her breast.

She shivered. "Yes."

"Then leave them to their own devices for once. Every so often you get a day off. It's the perks of being the boss."

"I should still get going," she said, trying to squirm away.

Dev leaned over her and planted his elbow on her far side. "Are we going to have to have that conversation all over again?"

"What conversation?"

"The one where we establish that we're both still very far from done with each other and that we should probably just keep going with this until—"

"Until what, the end of the week?" she threw it in with an attempt at flippancy. "You make it sound simple."

"Isn't it? We enjoy each other's company," he slid a hand along her hip, "we enjoy each other's bodies. What's the problem?"

"The problem is that I don't want to get involved. I like you, Dev, but I don't want to get tied up in a bad situation."

His eyes flashed then with a look she couldn't quite decipher. "Who says it's going to turn bad?"

Taylor swallowed. "Look, I've been married. Things were good, then we got married and they turned bad. You've been engaged. Things were good and then they turned bad. Maybe long-term commitments aren't a good thing for either of us."

"Committed pessimist, hmm?"

"A realist," she corrected.

"Hardly. Look, just because we're in bed together

doesn't mean we're locked into anything. Don't worry about tomorrow. Let's just enjoy today.''

She wanted badly to agree but it sounded too easy. ''Swear we'll stay away from the long-term stuff?''

''We'll take it day to day,'' he said. When her frown didn't abate, he gave her an exasperated look. ''Okay, how about this? I promise that I won't propose to you. Is that good enough?''

She nodded, still uneasy.

''Good.'' He moved one of his legs in between hers. ''Now let's get back to the part about enjoying one another's bodies.''

12

TAYLOR STARED INTO DEV'S kitchen, hands on her hips. "Normal people don't have sawhorses in their kitchens, you know," she remarked.

"They're useful."

"Or bare concrete floors. Sinks, though, they usually have sinks."

"I like to think of myself as a man who doesn't get caught up in convention," he said lightly.

She smiled. "So what are you going to do with it?"

"I'm going to move that wall over there back so that I can add a laundry room, and cut a pass through in this one so you can get to the dining room. That nook over there is going to be an area for a wine rack." He looked around as though he already saw it in front of him. "And the usual renovation stuff, rip out the old lath and plaster and hang new Sheetrock, refinish and reinstall the cabinets, add a venting system, new appliances, new flooring." He ticked them off on his fingers.

Taylor raised her eyebrows. "Sounds like you've got a job ahead of you. Did you know you were going to do all this when you bought the place?"

"Oh, yeah. I came into it planning to do a top to bottom renovation." Dev shrugged. "I'm a builder. That's what I do."

"Doesn't it ever get to be too much, building all day and then coming home to work on this place at night?"

"No." His eyes lit. "When you do a place like this, it's like you can hear it saying thank you. Come in here and look at this." He seized her hand and led her down a hall to where glass-paned French doors opened into the living room, a spacious, gracious room that was one of the few he'd finished. The brass and milk glass light fixture hung from an ornate ceiling medallion. On the hearth of the marble-topped fireplace sat an antique-looking brass fire screen. Bay windows overlooked the street and out into a side yard with a maple tree taller than the house. On the floor, warm swaths of glowing oak showed at the edge of the Persian rug. "This was covered in wall-to-wall carpeting when I bought the place. I didn't even know it was under there. I patched a few places and refinished it and look at it," he said, kneeling down to smooth a hand over the lustrous wood. "That's the kind of surprise that you get in a place like this. The kitchen cabinets are solid maple. Once I get the paint off and get them sanded down, they're going to be gorgeous."

Watching the satisfaction in his face made her heart stutter a bit. "You really love this place, don't you."

He looked suddenly bashful. "Shows that much, huh?"

"It's like it has a life and a voice of its own that only you can hear. I don't see how you could look at a new house after being in a place like this."

Dev snorted. "All Melissa wanted to do was sell it and buy a new one in a subdivision somewhere. Look at this." He pointed to the mantel and she stepped closer to look. The fuzzy sepia tone image showed gracefully ornate lines of a house so new that the shrubs and trees were still dwarfed. A horse and carriage sat alongside it, along with a man in a bowler hat and muttonchop whiskers. "I got this from the historical society. It's this house, about two years after it was built, or so they guess."

There was something magical about looking at the image and knowing that she stood inside the house nearly a century later. "It's like owning a little piece of the past."

"Like being entrusted with it, more like," Dev said, staring at the picture. "You take care of it while it's yours and pass it on."

"Do you ever mind all the work?"

He shrugged. "It's not all work. Tearing the walls out is kind of fun. I mean, when was the last time someone handed you a crowbar and told you to punch a hole in the wall?"

"You're joking, right?"

He waved her back toward the kitchen. "I told you I had to strip out the old lath and plaster. That was going to be my job for the weekend. Look." He picked up a clawed tool. "You give it a swing, let it bite into the wall and hook it back." A gaping hole appeared. He did it again and studs appeared. "Give it a try just once," he urged. "For the hell of it."

It did look like fun, she had to confess. Tentatively she took the tool from him and thumped it against the wall. It barely dented the plaster.

"Come on, put your back into it. Pick it up with both hands and really let 'er rip."

Taylor lifted it up and swung and the tool punched into the wall.

"Now give it a yank."

When she did, a section of the wall came loose.

"Now do it again."

She did, laughing and waving the plaster dust away from her face. "Well, this is a morning after like I've never had. Good thing I had jeans. Can we do it some more?"

He stared at her. "Are you serious?"

"Yeah. Like you said, how often does a person get to do something like this? Besides, if you don't get this done, you're never going to be able to cook again."

"That's not exactly a hardship." His tone was dry. "I wanted to spend time with you this weekend."

"So spend it with me," she said simply. "Teach me how to work on the house. It's like doing volunteer work for the historical society."

"Well, if you're serious, we should get you in long sleeves and a dust mask."

"Put me to work, chief."

THEY SAT FACING EACH OTHER on upended five-gallon paint buckets, drinking bottled water in the evening light. Taylor looked at Dev and smiled.

"What?" he asked.

"I'm just thinking now I know what you'll look like when you're seventy and your hair is white."

He shook his head and a drift of plaster dust fell out of it. "So how does it feel to be a homewrecker?" Dev pulled a rag out of his pocket and dampened it with water, then wiped it over her face to mop off the worst of the plaster. "Mmm, kabuki makeup."

"Is it me?" She tilted her head.

"I'm thinking a shower is probably a better move."

"You just wanted to get me naked so you can grope me."

"No—but now that you mention it," he said, looking at her consideringly.

Taylor unscrewed the cap from her bottle and took a swig of water. "That was fun, tearing things down."

He gave a short laugh. "It's always faster and easier than building them, that's for sure."

"But you like the building part best."

"It gives you something you can be proud of," he said, wiping the plaster off his own face.

It made her like him even more. "So what got you hooked on construction? Did you grow up building things?"

"Grow up building things?" Dev paused. "No. I was sixteen and I needed a job. Talked the foreman on a local site into hiring me as a cleanup boy. I stayed out of trouble and soaked up everything they'd let me and it kind of went from there."

What kind of sixteen-year-old "needed" a job, she wondered? "Why renovation? Did you grow up in an old house?"

He was silent long enough that she wondered if she'd said something wrong. "Yeah, I grew up in an old house. It was too far gone for renovating, though. Then again, our whole family was."

He'd opened the door. It took her little time to decide to walk through it. "In what way?"

"In just about every way you can think of," he said, elbows on his knees. "My mother left when I was about eight. We just came home from school one day and she was gone...." His voice trailed off.

"I'm so sorry," Taylor murmured, watching him closely. How would it have felt, she wondered, to come home and find an empty house, a mother who wasn't coming back? Unimaginable, she thought. For better or worse, her family was always there, one of the constants in her life.

"My dad never got over it," he said, picking up a broken piece of lath and tracing patterns in the drift of plaster on the bare concrete floor. "He never believed in anything after that, except maybe his bottle."

"How is he now?"

"Dead," he said abruptly. "Killed in an accident on the docks when I was about twenty."

For an instant, Taylor couldn't think what to say. "I'm sorry" seemed so inadequate. "He'd have been proud of the man you've become."

"I don't know." Dev examined the pattern of swirls he'd made between them. "We didn't exactly see eye to eye."

"That kind of thing matters less as time goes on and blood matters more."

"Maybe." He broke the lath in half and tossed the pieces into an oversize garbage can sitting to one side. "Anyway, it was a long time ago."

She hesitated, then took the leap. "Why did your mother leave?"

He shook his head. "I'm not sure any of us knew. I thought I did," he said reflectively. "When I was a kid I knew that she left because of my father. It was something he hadn't done. If he'd just tried, if he'd loved her enough, she'd have been happy enough to stay."

Her heart broke for that little boy, alone and confused. "But you don't believe that now?"

"I don't know what to believe. The earliest stuff I remember is us laughing and happy. I don't know if that was real or just the kiddie version of reality. Maybe that happened before life started tightening the thumbscrews on them. Two kids is a lot more work than one, you know." His voice drifted off into momentary silence. "It just seemed like the older I got, the more she was unhappy, with my dad, maybe, or with being a mom. Maybe she didn't like being settled down or she didn't like being broke. I think about it now and I figure she was probably mostly unhappy with herself, but she couldn't figure out how to leave that so she left us instead."

"Did you ever talk with your dad about it?"

Dev shook his head. "He pretty much shut down when she left. Anyway, I blamed him too much to ever have a conversation about it. By the time I'd stopped blaming him, he was dead."

"What about the rest of your family?"

"There isn't any worth mentioning except my sister, Mallory. She took it harder than I did when my mom left. She figured it was because of her."

"Kids often do."

He smiled faintly. "Not me. I figured Pop didn't love my mom enough or she'd have stayed." He gave a short laugh. "That's why I kept trying with Melissa. Every time we'd fight, I'd think that if I could just love her enough and help her, she'd get past her devils and it would work. I didn't want to quit." He fell silent and picked up another splinter of lath.

"I know about not wanting to quit," Taylor said softly.

"Yeah?"

She nodded. "That's my family rep. I'm the one who gets an idea and drops it."

"You haven't dropped your business," he pointed out.

"Yet. I think they're always waiting for me to. My grandmother left us all a little bit of money in a trust fund. My mother was appalled when I used some of mine to start the agency. She said I was throwing it away."

"But now you're profitable."

A corner of her mouth curved up. "They call it my little hobby."

He rubbed his knuckles against his jaw. "Tough crowd."

"I come from a family of overachievers…you know, doctor, lawyer, Indian chief?"

"And you were none of those, I take it?"

"I might have been interested in Indian chief if I'd gotten to wear feathers," she said with a faint smile. "No, I think they all love me, I'm just a little more…feckless than the others. They stuck with the plan, I followed my nose. And I did the unpardonable, by quitting school."

He raised his eyebrows. "Is that why you want to go back now?"

"Not really. I'm just ready to learn now. I wasn't then. Back then, I was only there because it was expected."

"If it didn't fit you, what's the point?"

If only the question had been that simple, she thought, remembering the acrimonious fights. "In my

family, if you don't have a degree, you're like some
sort of alien. Scientifically interesting, but not one of
them.''

"Everyone has to follow their own path." Dev
reached out to tangle his fingers with hers. "You were
smart to please yourself."

"Not so smart," she murmured, and the shadows
drifted into her eyes again.

"Why do you say that?" he asked, watching her
closely.

Taylor shook her head briskly. "Old baggage."

"Everybody's got baggage. It goes with the terri-
tory. It's not the baggage, it's how long you decide
to carry it."

And what had she done with hers, she wondered.
Let it weigh her down even as she tried to move on
with her life. Let it shadow her. Let it keep her in the
box Bennett had tried to build around her rather than
be herself. She hadn't really started to tread the final
road back to who she was until Mexico.

Until Dev, she realized, suddenly shaken. The ca-
sual lover she'd taken had wound himself far deeper
into her life than she'd ever thought possible.

Outside, a sudden breeze sent tree branches rattling
and scraping against the window.

Taylor shifted uneasily. There was no need to
panic, she reminded herself. They were only having
a light affair. No strings. Nothing permanent. She
cleared her throat. "Well, I'd say we could tear down
some more walls, but I think we've done enough for
today.''

Dev looked at her, then nodded. "I guess I can only
expect so much slave labor before I have to give some

compensation. How about if I take you out to dinner, instead?''

"Sure," she said distractedly and went into the downstairs bathroom to wash her hands.

IT WAS HIS FIRM POLICY never to ask a person what they were thinking, but the play of expressions he'd just seen on her face made him wonder. First shadowed, then pensive, then simply startled. What was going on in her head? Not, he reminded himself as he began picking up construction detritus, that it was any of his business. He didn't have license to pry.

And yet, somehow that fact just made him want to know all the more.

"I think after making you work on my house all weekend that I owe you a weekend away somewhere," he said, almost before he realized he was going to say it. "What do you say to getting out of town for a few days?"

Taylor came out of the bathroom drying her hands on a frayed blue towel. "Where did that come from? Don't you want to finish your house?"

He just chuckled. "Darlin', this house isn't going to be finished until sometime next year. I'm in no hurry. You said you'd never been to Newport, and I'd think you'd like it. Do you have plans next weekend?"

She tilted her head and looked at him. "Why do I get the feeling that there's a catch?"

"I suppose there is," he said sheepishly. "My sister's getting married next weekend in Newport. I want you to go with me."

"A wedding."

"Uh-huh."

"You just want company on the drive, right?"

"Maybe I don't want to go without sex for two days," he said lightly.

A slow smile spread over her face. "That would be a hardship, now that you mention it."

"See. I'm trying to be proactive."

"It's impressive."

"I'm a trained professional. Don't try this at home."

She gave him an appraising look. "I don't know. You know bringing me to a wedding makes me the hot topic for your family."

"That would be my sister, remember?"

"Still, if you want me to be an escort for you, you're going to have to make it worth my while," she said, amusement ripe in her voice.

A corner of his mouth twitched. "And how do I do that?"

"Well, I don't know. What does it involve? Is this one of those all-weekend-long wedding orgies?"

"Not if my sister has anything to say about it. There's a rehearsal dinner Saturday night and the wedding is Sunday. Other than that, we can do what we please," he said, raising her hand to his lips. "Oh, and I have to pick up a bed."

"Is that a Carson wedding tradition?"

Dev laughed. "No. She doesn't need it now that she's getting married and I do."

"Well, the bare metal frame you've got upstairs has its own charm, I suppose, but you're probably right. Must be some bed if you're prepared to haul it all the way down from Newport."

"She claims it's special."

"How?" She wrinkled her brow. "Does it have a vibrator in it or something?"

"I don't know," he said with a shrug. "You'll have to ask her when you meet her."

"I can see it now. 'Nice to meet you. Let's talk about that bed of yours.'"

"You want to talk about my bed?" he asked, sweeping her close.

"Well, now that you mention it," she whispered against his mouth.

13

———

TAYLOR YAWNED AS SHE STUDIED the paperwork before her. Negotiating discount agreements with resort chains wasn't exactly scintillating stuff, but it was vital to her business. If she closed on this one, which involved many of the properties she'd visited weeks before, she'd be able to offer her clients juicy rates and some of the most gorgeous properties around.

Including Cozumel. Her eyes softened and she reached across her desk to touch the tiny furled shell Dev had given her as she left the resort. Nearly a week had passed since they'd rekindled their romance, and if anything she'd had even more fun than she had in Mexico. They packed the days with work, the nights with fun and passion. She'd had nearly everything she could want.

Except sleep.

She yawned again as the light flashed on her phone and she picked up the handset. "Taylor DeWitt."

"Alan Champlin here."

She blinked at the name of her competitor and would-be buyer. "Hi, Alan, how are you?"

"Not as good as you must be. I understand congratulations are in order."

"I'm sorry?"

"Pace-Miller as a corporate client? Your agency is

moving up in the world." He sounded amused and just the slightest bit envious.

"We're pleased with it." And she'd have bet her bottom dollar that Champlin Travel had gone after Pace-Miller with everything they had. The fact that she'd won out, even against the resources of the glossy chain gave her a warm glow of satisfaction.

"You've been sitting on my offer for six weeks."

"You told me to take my time and think about it. I have."

"And?"

She sighed. As much as she'd been tempted by the idea of school and trying something different, she knew she needed to stick with the agency.

"I appreciate the offer, but I'm going to have to decline."

"It's a generous offer. Do you mind me asking why?"

She paused. Tempting though Champlin's offer was, it would make her a little cog in a vast machine. Running an office in a mall somewhere hardly compared to running her own agency and being free to take risks and shoot for bigger things. "I guess I'm happier being my own boss."

"You'd be in a position of authority," he hastened to point out. "You could run that unit you're in now, or even several locations."

But that would just be people management, not the wheeling and dealing she craved. "I like what I'm doing now," she said, choosing her words carefully. It didn't do to forget that she was talking to a competitor.

"What do you like about it? What do you want to

make this package go? No guarantees, but it would help me to know.''

Taylor searched for diplomacy. "Look, Alan, thanks for your interest, but I think I'm more likely to do the type of work I enjoy at my own agency."

"You're getting more and more involved with the corporate clients," Champlin said thoughtfully.

"I'm really not comfortable having a strategy conversation with you."

"Just tell me this," he persisted. "If I come up with a different offer, will you at least listen to it?"

"Boy, you really are desperate for this location, aren't you," she laughed.

"Can you blame me? But I also want you on board. You know how to get the job done."

The compliment gave her a little buzz of pleasure before she tamped it down and glanced at the clock in the corner of her computer screen. "I appreciate your interest, Alan, really, but understand that I'm not fishing here. I'm happy with what I'm doing."

"All I'm asking is will you listen?"

She sighed. "Sure, I'll listen."

"Great. Have a good week, then."

Taylor hung up the phone feeling strangely unsettled. She walked to the door of her office and leaned against the doorjamb, staring out at the nearly finished space. It looked clean and professional, with her trio of agents behind their desks. Nicole had what looked like a young stockbroker sitting in her visitor chair, leafing through a brochure as she quoted him numbers. It was a success, and she'd built it up from scratch.

Maybe her family was right about her, she thought gloomily. Building a successful business wasn't enough. She craved new challenges. Turning her back on the agency wasn't possible, though, not if she wanted to hold on to her self-respect. She couldn't just quit again, and yet she itched to stretch herself beyond what she'd already accomplished. She craved a job that had her engaged every single day when she came in, and now that the agency was ticking along, it no longer quite fit the bill.

She sighed and went back to her desk. The thing to do was focus on what worked and resign herself to the rest, she thought, toying with the shell again.

And in the meantime, jump Dev Carson's bones as often as possible.

RILEY PARKED HIS TRUCK behind the scarred tan construction trailer and got out. The gutter was littered with gravel, bits of cement and Sheetrock. They'd need to sweep up the street when they finished the job the following week, he thought, heading for the trailer before starting onto the job site to look for Dev.

The cell phone on his belt tweeted and vibrated. He glanced at the display, shuddering as he saw his mother's number. It was a conversation he had no desire to have.

It was a conversation he couldn't avoid.

"Caldwell," he said briefly.

"I've left messages for you at work, I've left messages for you at home. What does a person have to do to get in touch with you?"

"I was going to call you, Ma," Riley protested.

"Don't you try that one on me. I paged you twice yesterday and you didn't answer. If your secretary hadn't given me this number, I'd still be tracking you down. What have things come to when a mother has to get her son's cell phone number from his secretary, that's what I'd like to know.''

Ignoring her was the safest course, he thought. ''So how are things?''

''Depends what things you mean. Your father and I are fine. You forgot to send your niece a birthday card, by the way.''

He closed his eyes and cursed mentally. ''I'll send one off today.''

''That doesn't fix it.''

''Ma, Stephanie just turned a year old. The card isn't for her, it's for Elaine.''

''Well, obviously,'' she said in a tone that said she was doubting his intelligence. ''Stephanie can't read yet.''

He sighed. ''Is that what you called about?''

''No, I called to find out what you're doing about your cousin.''

''Nothing, right now.''

''You know she's crying her eyes out over that clod you're in business with? Your uncle's about ready to come over and give him a piece of his mind.''

''Ma, it's between Melissa and Dev. Tell Uncle Carl to keep out of it.''

''Well, that's what I keep telling him. Do you know how much they lost in deposits alone on that wedding? In my day, young men didn't call off their engagements without an explanation to anyone. It's outrageous.''

''I'm sure Melissa knows what it's about, Ma,'' Riley said with a sinking heart.

''And what would that be? She says she doesn't have the first idea. It's tearing her to pieces.''

"It's between them. I don't know and I don't want to know," he lied. It wasn't entirely a lie, actually. He *didn't* want to know, except that he'd been in the hall behind Dev when his friend had opened the door to discover Melissa and her paramour in flagrante delicto.

His mother gave a harrumph. "You could ask. You could talk to the man. Melissa is just a mess over this. Lord only knows why, but she wants him back, or at least to know why. It seems to me that a cousin who cared about family might at least talk with his friend and try to do something about it."

Riley rubbed his forehead. "Ma, I can't tell him to do something he doesn't want to do."

"I'm not saying you have to tell him to do anything. Maybe just get them together. If it really is love, that's all it will take."

"It's not my place."

"Blood is thicker than water, Riley Kendall Caldwell," she said sharply. "That's the way I raised you."

"Ma," he protested.

"Don't you 'Ma' me. You do your duty by your family and that's final."

The click left him holding the phone and cursing in the street.

14

NOISE, A CROWD. These were her first impressions.
The long, narrow room was lined with warm wood
and dotted with vintage movie posters. At the back,
the room opened up to a space where a band played
hard and nasty roots rock to the delight of the surging
mass of people on the dance floor. Those of the hip,
youngish crowd not dancing clustered around small
tables or standing along the walls, leaned on the
scarred wooden ledges. Behind the bar, the staff
shoved bottles and glasses across the polished wood
as fast as customers could order them.

"Welcome to Bad Reputation," Dev shouted.

"You own this?" Taylor asked.

He shook his head. "My sister does. I just threw
some money in to help her get started."

A brass bell clanged and Taylor looked toward the
bar to see a frankly stunning brunette kneeling on the
bar chug down a pint glass of beer while the circle
of people around her clapped and egged her on. When
she finished it, she clasped her hands over her head
like a prize fighter.

"Where's your sister?" Taylor asked.

A grin flashed across his face. "Well," he began.

Just then, the woman looked up. With a whoop,
she jumped off the bar and pushed her way through
the crowd to throw her arms around Dev's neck and

give him a smacking kiss. "Where have you been? I expected you hours ago."

Dev laughed. "Taylor DeWitt, meet my sister, Mallory."

THE REDHEADED BARTENDER named Fiona poured drinks for them as they leaned on the bar. "So I thought, Mallory go to her wedding day without a hen night? 'Tisn't right,'' she explained, her Irish accent making the words dance. "So we decided to make it spur of the moment."

"Hen night?" Taylor repeated blankly, taking the beer that Fiona handed her.

"Bachelorette party," Mallory supplied over Fiona's shoulder. "Ignoring the fact that the bar's open for business."

"Well, then, you'd be at a public bar if it were a regular bachelorette party, then, wouldn't you?" Fiona replied smartly.

"But I wouldn't be trying to run it at the same time."

"She's a little bit of a control junkie," Dev put in genially, reaching out for his own beer.

"I've seen that, to be sure," Fiona said. "So she can't trust us to run it for her while she has a last celebration?"

"It's been about six years since I've gotten drunk, Fiona," Mallory said dryly. "I don't intend to start again two days before my wedding."

"I guess you'll have to pace yourself, then, won't you? Now go round and talk to your brother and his guest," Fiona admonished. "We'll tend to things."

Mallory hopped onto the bar, pivoted so her feet pointed out into the room, and landed in front of Taylor and Dev. "I'd say it's not usually this much of a mob scene, but I'd be lying—thank God." Behind her, the band broke into the cover of a Smashmouth tune.

"I like it," Taylor said, unable to stop herself from swaying a little to the music. "It's fun. I went to a bar about this crazy back when I lived in Providence, only we used to dance on the tables."

Mallory's eyes flashed with humor. "Well, we used to do our share of dancing on the furniture around here, too. You like dancing, stick around. These guys mostly do covers, but they're fun. We'll have to see if we can find you a partner."

"Hey, I dance," Dev put in.

Mallory sniffed. "Since when?"

"I can vouch for it," Taylor put in.

"*My* brother?"

Taylor nodded. "He's good at it. If they play the right kind of beat, we'll have to get him to take you out there and spin you around."

Mallory gave her a speculative look. "You don't say. That sounds great," she said with sudden warmth.

The next moment she was swept away by a dark-haired stranger with the look of a pirate. Since Dev didn't seem inclined to jump him, she figured it was probably Mallory's fiancé, soon to be her husband.

He and Mallory took their time getting reacquainted, but eventually they pried themselves apart and he shook with Dev. Then he turned to her, sticking out his hand. "Shay O'Connor."

"Taylor DeWitt," she said bemusedly.

Just then, Fiona stepped onto the bar, drawing whoops from the crowd and ringing the bell until everyone quieted down. "Thank you. Now, for those of you who don't know, tonight is in the way of a celebration." A chorus of whistles drowned out her words and she waited for them to end. "What I mean is that it's more of a celebration than usual. Can we have the guest of honor up on the bar?"

Mallory rolled her eyes, but Fiona started a measured clap and others joined in until the whole room echoed with it. Dev pushed at Mallory's shoulder. Finally she caved and climbed up on the bar next to Fiona to give an exaggerated bow.

"Now Mallory here, your proprietor, is getting married on Sunday," Fiona announced gaily.

In the crowd, a guy in his mid-twenties threw his hand over his heart. "No, don't do it," he shouted.

"Anyway, we're celebrating tonight," Fiona continued, ignoring him. "And just so she doesn't forget the roots of her success, we've got a special song for the bride-to-be." She turned to point to the band and they swung into a cover of the Georgia Satellites' "Keep Your Hands to Yourself." Fiona turned to Mallory. "One last dance for the bride," she shouted, and the room erupted.

The lyrics were the heart cry of a frustrated swain getting rebuffed repeatedly by an altar-bent girlfriend. As the infectious beat filled the room, more and more people on the floor began dancing. The other bartenders climbed up onto the polished wood and began swaying to the beat. Mallory pantomimed the story in her dance, verse after verse, laughing down at Shay, who stood at her feet.

Mallory sang, crossing her arms in front of her.

Shay put a hand over his heart.

But Mallory just tossed her head.

The room erupted as the band segued into another song. Taylor laughed and danced in place next to Dev. Then Mallory looked down at her and beckoned. "Get on up here and dance if you want to."

Taylor glanced at Dev and Shay talking to one another. Why not, she thought. Why not? She stepped over to push herself up on the bar. Dev raised his eyebrows, then raised his glass to her. She stood up, swaying a little until she got her balance, and then began to snap her fingers and join the party.

THE MIDMORNING SUN the next day made Taylor glad she had her dark glasses. Not, of course, that she'd had more than a drink or two the night before, but dancing away the hours had taken it out of her more than she remembered. And what foolish humanitarian impulse had led her to volunteer herself and Dev to help get Shay's tavern decorated for the rehearsal dinner, she would never remember.

The warm, bright pub charmed her immediately. Sunlight streamed in through the enormous windows that ran around two walls. Whereas Mallory's bar had the feel of youth and energy, this one held a quiet comfort and ease all its own.

Or probably did on days when a handful of harried people weren't trying to arrange chairs, smooth tablecloths, set out flowers, hang decorations and generally transform the room.

"We've almost got the garlands up," Mallory said from where she stood on a chair, looking just the slightest bit tense to Taylor's eagle eye. "Someone's got to go get the wine, though."

"It's a pub," Shay said mildly. "People are going to expect ale."

"It's a sit-down dinner," she corrected distractedly, bounding down and moving her chair. "People
are going to want the option of wine. Besides, we
need the wine for the wedding dinner."

He relented. "Dev and I can go get it while we're
out."

Dev looked at him blankly. "When we're out
where?"

"Getting the tuxes. Did you think they were just
going to appear on their own?"

Dev rolled his eyes. "Oh, yeah, hell, I forgot all
about it."

"I figured you did. Come on."

"Hang on. Taylor, you want me to drop you off at
the hotel?"

Mallory glanced up. "Leave her here with us.
We'll get her hanging garland and keep her enter-
tained until you guys get back."

"Taylor?"

How bad could it be, she thought. "Go ahead. I'll
be fine and I can always walk back to the hotel if I
want."

"She means if she decides she's tired of being run
about by a madwoman like Mallory," Fiona put in.

"I'll be fine," she repeated.

"I STILL SAY THIS WOULD HAVE been more fun if
we'd taken your bike," Dev said as he got out of
Shay's truck in the parking lot of the tux shop.

"You try putting six cases of wine on the back of
a motorcycle and see how far you get," Shay said
dryly.

"It's a good thing you're getting married. You've
obviously lost your sense of adventure already."

Shay's only response was a snort as he slammed his door.

"You as excited about wearing rented clothes as I am?" Dev asked as they walked up to the shop.

"Speak for yourself. I own mine."

Dev looked at him with a raised eyebrow. "You planning a lifestyle change I don't know about, Cary?"

Shay shrugged. "I figure, she's getting a special dress. It's the least I can do to get a wedding suit." He opened the door to the shop.

Inside, silver mannequins posed in the latest men's formal wear. "So what did you guys pick out for me?" Dev asked, scanning over the array of vests pinned up on the wall behind the cash register. "Just what exactly is the well-dressed best man wearing these days?"

Shay spoke to the man behind the counter and turned back to Dev.

"Maybe salmon-pink tails? What do you think?"

The clerk returned. "Your suits are in your dressing rooms, gentlemen. If you'll just follow me?"

When they met in front of the mirrors a few minutes later, Dev was in a classic tuxedo and cummerbund, while Shay wore a tux with a silver brocade vest.

"Nice threads," Dev said, looking him up and down.

"They seem to fit," Shay said, checking it out in the mirror.

"Amazing what they can do with Velcro these days," Dev added.

The clerk reappeared. "Is everything all right?"

"We're good to go," Shay said. "If you can pack them up we'll be all set."

They changed and milled around in the front, waiting for the clerk to bring their clothing up front. "So what do you think, bud, you ready for this?" Dev asked as he fingered the white scarf that hung around the neck of a tuxedoed mannequin.

Shay nodded. "Yeah, I am. You?"

"I think I'm putting my sister into good hands."

"I'm sure your sister would point out that she didn't need to be in anyone's hands," Shay said dryly.

"You're coming in on the bar, though."

"Just to run the music side of it. She's heading up the rest of it." Shay gave Dev a curious look. "Are you okay with that? Do you want me to buy you out?"

"Hell, no," Dev said dismissively. "I trust you guys to make me an exorbitant amount of money. I figure I'll retire on it and live on my boat."

Shay gave a short laugh. "You always were an optimist, weren't you?" He took the garment bag proffered by the clerk.

"When it comes to you, buddy, there's no reason not to be." Dev's expression turned serious as he pushed open the door and they walked to the truck. "You and Mal are going to work, I think."

Shay grinned and opened his door. "I think so, too. It's been about a week since she's threatened to strangle me, so I figure we're doing well."

"That's my Mal," Dev said fondly.

"So what about you?" Shay asked. "What's with you and Taylor?"

Dev shrugged uncomfortably and concentrated on

fastening his seat belt. "Nothing much. We like each other, we get along great. We're just letting it run and playing it by ear."

"Yeah, I can see how Melissa would scare you off of anything serious for a while."

"No, it's not that. We just agreed that we'd keep it light."

"Whatever works," Shay said mildly. "Although I can't see what someone who looks that good would want with you."

Dev raised an eyebrow. "Someone who looks that good? Aren't you supposed to be marrying my sister tomorrow?"

A ridiculous grin spread over Shay's face. "Yeah, I am, aren't I?" He pushed his sunglasses up on his nose and backed his truck out of the spot.

"So what made you sure about all this?"

"Sure about Mallory or sure about getting married?"

"Both."

Shay shrugged. "Well, first it was that I couldn't get her off my mind. And whenever something happened, she was the first one I wanted to tell. Every time I thought about the future, I saw her there, so it just sort of made sense. Still does." He stopped at a traffic light and gave Dev a curious look. "So are we talking about me or about you?"

Dev watched a man walk out of a doughnut shop laden with boxes. "I don't know. After what happened with Melissa, I can't say I trust anything I feel. Still…"

"Still what?"

He stared moodily out the window. "I know I didn't start into this thing with Taylor looking for anything special. And she's so gun-shy, we practically had to write out a contract that we wouldn't get serious. But it feels good, in a way it never has for me. Like night and day compared to Melissa. Being with Taylor is…well, being with her is better than being alone.''

Shay snorted as they began moving again. ''Now there's a ringing endorsement.''

''No, you don't understand. I like being alone. Even with Melissa, I kind of liked it, the nights we'd be apart.'' They drove along a stretch of waterfront with a beach club complex of cabanas overlooking the ocean. ''It was a lot more peaceful, you know? Melissa was always a lot of work, especially by the end. It was only when she wasn't around that I could just hang.'' He paused. ''But it's not like that with Taylor. I don't feel like I have to *do* anything. It's easy, the same as being alone.''

Shay followed the road when it veered left, turning past a tavern with an old mural of Roger Clemens winding up for a pitch. The mural still showed The Rocket wearing a Red Sox cap, Dev noticed in amusement. An expression of cost savings or fandom, he wondered.

''Have you told Taylor any of this?''

Dev shook his head. ''It's too new. Besides, I tried the long-term thing with Melissa and it blew up in my face. Who's to say it wouldn't again?''

''Well, if you haven't even talked with her about it, you're probably getting ahead of yourself thinking long-term. But you shouldn't let Melissa poison the rest of your life.''

''It's not that I don't believe in long-term involvement. I do. But before I put myself on the line again with someone, I need to know I'm doing it for the right reasons and not just chasing after some fantasy.''

"Well, let me ask you this. Have you ever met anyone else that was better than being alone?''

He pretended to think, but he already knew the answer. "The man gets engaged and he thinks he's an expert on relationships.''

MALLORY STARED AT THE CARDS, tapping her fingers restlessly. "I'll raise you two and call,'' she said, pushing a pair of M&M's into the center of the table and turning up her cards to show three jacks.

Fiona groaned and tossed her cards down.

"Sorry, guys,'' Taylor said, showing her flush and scooping the pile of M&M's toward her.

"I can't believe my brother brought a card shark with him,'' Mallory muttered.

They sat around her coffee table. On the television, Myrna Loy and William Powell traded bon mots in *After the Thin Man.* The scent of baking brownies perfumed the air.

"Aren't you glad we talked you into leaving the pub to the caterers?'' Fiona asked.

Mallory took a drink of Coke and grabbed a chip from the bowl that sat at her knee. "You're such a good influence, Fee. How did I ever get along without you?''

"Haven't a clue. Perhaps it's time to talk about that raise?'' she said hopefully.

The front buzzer rang and Mallory jumped up lightly to answer it. They heard her feet clattering down the staircase that led down into the bar and the door to the street that she shared with it.

"So is she nervous, do you think?" Taylor asked Fiona.

"Maybe a little," Fiona guessed. "She wasn't any pushover for Shay, I'll tell you that. Mallory's not shy about keeping the jury out until she's sure. She seems sure about you," Fiona said unexpectedly.

Taylor gave her a quizzical glance. "Sure about me how?"

"Well, I wouldn't know, of course. But you're here, aren't you? Mallory doesn't let people into her home unless she likes them. Dev's ex-fiancée, for example, would never have been here."

"Mallory didn't like her?"

"Loathed her," Fiona said cheerfully. "Thought that she was going to lead Dev a miserable life. She was never so happy as when he called off the engagement."

The door to the front stairway opened. "Looks like Shay and I can get married after all," Mallory announced, stepping into the room. "The missing bridesmaid has arrived. Becka, meet Fiona and Taylor. Becka used to be my neighbor in Massachusetts. Becka, Fiona is currently the light of Shay's brother's life."

"And your shift manager," Fiona put in tartly.

"And my highly talented and valued shift manager," Mallory smiled. "Taylor came up with my brother for the wedding."

The redhead that walked in with Mallory gave a smile. In contrast to Fiona's fiery auburn curls, she had short, deep red hair with a fringe of bangs that only focused attention on her enormous green cat eyes. Something about the sharp-pointed chin and full cheekbones made Taylor think of a fox, a vixen peering out from the woods.

"Hi, guys," Becka said, sketching a wave. "Whatcha doing?"

"Taylor's currently cleaning us out of M&M's," Mallory said dryly. "Grab a seat, let me get you a drink and we can deal you in. Where'd you leave Mace, anyway?"

"He's at the hotel looking at scouting reports or something. Spring training. I had to pry him loose from Florida with a crowbar," Becka said, sinking down on a pile of pillows on the floor.

"Becka's married to a baseball jock," Mallory explained, heading to the kitchen.

"Don't bring me any of that sugary junk," Becka called. "I'll take water if you don't have anything else."

Mallory reappeared with a glass. "A good guest drinks what they're given."

"A good hostess caters to her guests," Becka countered.

"Most guests aren't so finicky," Mallory said, handing her the drink. "Taylor and Fiona don't have a problem with soda."

"I'm not finicky," Becka said hotly and took a sip of her drink. "I just don't…" A beatific smile spread over her face. "Lime seltzer water!"

"You were saying?" Mallory asked, joining the group sprawled around the coffee table.

"I worship you. I can't believe I doubted you. I'm unworthy."

"True. But it was nothing," Mallory said modestly.

"Well, let's have a toast to the bride-to-be," Becka

announced, raising her glass. "To Mallory and Shay, here's hoping they'll be blissfully happy together, and to the magic bed for getting them that way."

"I think Shay and I get some of the credit," Mallory argued.

"And to me," Becka added, ignoring her, "for giving Mallory the bed."

Taylor darted looks at the two of them. "What bed?" she asked. "The one you're giving to Dev?"

Becka choked on her seltzer water.

THEY STOOD IN MALLORY'S bedroom, admiring the satiny carved wood of the four-poster.

"It's gorgeous," Taylor said, running a hand up the carved bedpost. "How can you part with it?"

"Shay's already got a bed that he inherited from his great-grandfather," Mallory said. "Besides, I'm superstitious."

"What does that mean?"

Mallory exchanged a look with Becka. "You might say I don't want to interrupt the chain."

Taylor looked at them with resignation. "All right, what's the joke? You guys are dying to tell it."

"It's not a joke," Becka said, sitting down on the mattress and bouncing a little. "The bed's just a…a good luck charm, I guess. A friend of mine bought it. A couple of weeks later she met the guy who's now her husband. They had two beds, so she gave it to me. A couple of weeks after that, I met someone."

"This is sounding a lot like one of those chain letters," Taylor put in.

"Yeah, well ask her who this someone is," Mallory said. "Only Mr. Baseball Star, Fifty Most Beautiful People Mace Duvall someone."

Taylor goggled at Becka. "You're married to Mace Duvall?"

Becka batted her eyes. "Like I said, it's a magic bed."

"I'll say."

Mallory leaned against the footboard. "I'll just point out that she didn't tell me any of these details until after I'd already gotten the thing moved in. I didn't know I was kissing my singledom goodbye. I wasn't looking to get married, you know."

"Oh, you didn't believe in it even when I did tell you," Becka said impatiently. "Anyway, it's not like you're being tortured into marrying Shay or anything. I saw you making goo-goo eyes at each other when we were here before."

"I'm just turning nearsighted, that's all."

"Yeah, very nearsighted, like you want Shay near you all the time."

They grinned at each other, then Mallory turned back to Taylor. "So anyway, understand you're near this bed at your own risk. We can't be responsible for what happens."

Fiona gave the bed a speculative look and sat down on the mattress beside Becka.

"I'll consider myself warned," Taylor said, resisting the urge to roll her eyes.

"Laugh all you want," Becka said mildly. "The bed is three for three right now."

In the other room, a timer began to beep.

"What's that?" Becka asked.

Fiona's eyes glittered. "Fudge brownies."

"Oh."

"You probably won't want any, though," Mallory

told her. "It's not health food or anything. It's got white flour, refined sugar, all that disgusting stuff."

"I'll sacrifice for the sake of my friends," Becka said nobly. "Maybe I'd better go get them out of the oven."

"I'll help," Fiona added and they were gone in a brownie stampede.

Taylor started to follow them until she heard Mallory call her name. She turned.

Mallory stood, her hand still on the smooth, polished wood of the footboard. "I almost didn't give it to Dev, you know. I wouldn't have if it had been a couple of months ago, when he was still with that head case."

"You didn't like her, I take it?"

"I don't like anyone who makes someone I care for unhappy." Mallory frowned. "She pushed his buttons like he was an elevator. No one should get away with treating someone like that, especially when they give lip service to caring for them. Especially not when the person getting hurt is one of my people."

Taylor nodded. "I can understand feeling like that." She hesitated. "You know that Dev and I aren't serious, don't you?"

"He cares about you, though. It shows when you're together. And you care about him."

"Well, yeah, I think he's really wonderful. I just don't want to give you the wrong impression. I came up here with him just to keep him company. We're not looking at a future or anything."

To her discomfort, Mallory began to laugh. "Whatever you say." She threw an arm around Taylor's shoulders. "Just don't forget to pick up the bed on your way home."

15

SPOONS TAPPED AGAINST THE sides of water glasses, filling the room with a musical ringing that signified the time for speeches. Taylor looked to the head of the table where Aidan O'Connor, Shay's father stood up to speak. The next afternoon, at the wedding reception, Dev would give the toast as best man. This night, though, the rehearsal dinner, belonged to Shay's father.

Wedding traditions had always seemed so lovely and moving to her. She couldn't say now why she felt so ill at ease. It wasn't as though she hadn't been involved in a wedding since her own marriage had imploded. Why, then, was her stomach in knots?

Aidan cleared his throat. "I want to welcome you all here. Tomorrow, we'll celebrate Mallory and Shay's wedding, so let me get in a word or two before things get crazy. First, I just want to say how proud Gillian and I are of our son and his choice of a wife. Shay's become all we could have hoped for, and he's chosen himself a smart, capable and lovely bride."

"And one that won't take any nonsense from him," Gillian put in, to the accompaniment of laughter.

Taylor's mind went back to her own rehearsal dinner. It hadn't been held at a warm, family establishment but amid the slick, anonymous gloss of a country club. Instead of warmth and well wishing, the words of Bennett's father's speech were spun through with sarcasm, cheap shots at Bennett's expense, and a barb or two for her enjoyment. It should, perhaps, have given her a glimmer of what was to come. At the time, she'd simply held Bennett's hand and tried to smile.

"Anyway, I know these two are going to have a great marriage and a great life."

She'd known that she and Bennett were going to have a great life. She remembered sitting there, raising her glass for the toasts, impatient to get it all over with and get on with the business of real life. Foolish and naive, in the way only the young could be, perhaps. Oh, but she'd learned her lesson soon after. Bennett had taught her everything she needed to know about foolish dreams...

Her stomach churned and she rose.

Dev touched her hand. "Are you okay?"

"I have to run to the rest room," she managed to say, though it felt like bands of iron were tightening around her throat.

"Hurry back," he whispered, and kissed her hand.

SHE WAS ALMOST PATHETICALLY glad to see their room at the bed and breakfast again, the teal walls, the high bed with its inviting pile of quilts where she could tumble into sleep and perhaps dream. The toasts were done, the light conversations were over. They'd packed Mallory and Shay off to their last nights as single people.

All Taylor wanted was a long, hot soak in the tub, a fire, and a chance to escape the thoughts that had been chasing her all night.

Dev laid the key down on the cherrywood dresser and hung up their coats. Taylor fled for the bathroom. She took her time in the tub, then brushing her teeth, brushing her hair, changing into a negligee. It was late and they'd had a big dinner. Perhaps he'd be asleep by the time she was finished, she thought.

No such luck. Instead he was sitting in a tufted brocade love seat, staring directly at her when she came out of the bathroom.

Taylor stiffened, then relaxed. "Sorry, I didn't think you'd still be up."

He looked at her for a moment, then picked up the box of matches on the fireplace. "I figured we could start a fire, enjoy it a little before we go to bed," he said neutrally, bending to the fireplace. She heard the snick of the match against the strike pad and saw flame hiss up. "So what's going on?" Dev asked without turning.

Why was she surprised he'd known something was up? And how could she convince him it wasn't? "I'm just tired. Long day," she said, throwing in a fake yawn.

He took his time with the log, lighting the paper wrapper at several points along its length. "You were gone a long time at dinner during the toasts." He drew the brass mesh fire screen closed.

"It's okay," Taylor said dismissively.

He rose, setting the matches back on the mantel. "No, it is definitely not okay," he said, shaking his head. "You've been looking like death all night. What's going on?"

When he looked at her this time, she had nowhere to escape. When he caught her hands and drew her to the love seat, she was trapped. Perhaps if she gave him part of the truth, it would be enough. "Being at the rehearsal dinner tonight, the toasting, it just took me back."

"More like it made you see a ghost."

"The Ghost Of Weddings Past." She tried for a smile that failed miserably. "Maybe it did. I was married before."

"And divorced. I know."

He pulled her over to lean against him, and the warmth of his arms around her thawed some of the chill that had crept into her bones. And somehow, it made it easier to speak, staring into the dancing flames of the fire. "No, you don't know. You can't imagine."

He pressed his lips to her temple. "Tell me," he said softly.

She hesitated. "Before we were married, he was great. Sweet, romantic…he made me feel special, like he believed in me. He told me not to listen to what my family said. He gave me the nerve to stand up against them. I mean, my parents had a fit when I told them I was quitting school to get married. Even after they met Bennett, they thought we should wait. I didn't want to, neither did he. I finally wore my parents down. I was so happy. I thought everything was perfect." She swallowed around the lump in her throat. "And then he changed."

"What did he do to you?" Dev asked, his voice low, threaded through with a hint of danger.

"He never hit me. He never had to. He could slice you to ribbons with his tongue," Taylor said, fighting to sound matter-of-fact. "It was all so subtle, though. If he'd ever gotten physical, I could have left him. Instead it was just the off and on attacks. Sometimes he'd be sweet, and then wham, he'd just..." She trailed off. The fireplace log hissed and sent up a small shower of sparks.

"Why didn't you leave?"

"Who, me? Taylor the quitter?" She looked at him bleakly. "I was ashamed. Everyone had tried to get me to stop on my way to the altar, but I knew best. Now, I'd be coming back and saying I'd been wrong."

"There are worse things, especially when you're living with abuse."

"I tried to tell my mother once. She told me it was time I learned to live with my decisions and not run out when things got difficult. She thought Bennett was a good man. Everybody did. He was the model husband in public. It was only in private..." Her voice cracked.

"What finally happened?"

Taylor sighed and let her head fall back onto his shoulder. "I'd gone to visit my parents, or so Bennett thought. He always hated for me to go places alone. He liked to be along to monitor things."

"I'm sure."

"I'd lied to him, though. I'd gone to my parents' for a day or two and then I went to visit my girlfriend Jody from college." She swallowed. "I came home early. I thought it might make things easier with Bennett if I did. Maybe he'd be less angry. It was supposed to be a surprise."

Instead she'd been the one to get the surprise.

How easily she could still remember coming in quietly through the kitchen door, hearing voices and loud music. "Oh, yeah, baby, touch yourself there again," he'd said, an instant before Taylor had burst through the door to find a woman doing a striptease for him. Or mostly a tease, since the better part of her clothing appeared to have been stripped off long before.

"I found him with a woman. It was pretty obvious." Taylor blinked dry eyes. It wasn't tears that the memory brought to her now, but burning shame that she'd wasted so much time on trying to please Bennett.

"What did he do?"

"Tried to blame it on me, of course." She'd driven him to it, he'd raged. He was under too much pressure, working too hard. If she'd been a better wife, he wouldn't have been vulnerable to the lure of another woman.

"Another time, it might have worked. I wasn't in real great shape emotionally by that point. But I'd just been with Jody. She'd reminded me of who I really was, and I had just enough in me to leave him." That night had been a blur, driving down the New Jersey Turnpike in the rain, leaving behind New York and all she'd once thought she wanted from life.

"He didn't make it easy, I'm sure."

"He didn't," she agreed. "But I had backing. Infidelity was something I could take to my parents. I'm not sure they ever really understood the rest, but I got out. I got out," she repeated.

"You didn't just get out, you made a success of yourself. You've got so much to be proud of." He tightened his arms around her. "You know someone like Bennett is sick. That's no reflection on you."

"It is a reflection on me. I didn't see it." She stared at the crown molding that ran around the ceiling, neat and tidy, covering up cracks. It was a shame they didn't have crown moldings for the soul. "You don't understand. I thought he was the love of my life, and he turned out to be a monster. What does that say about my judgment? How can I trust anything I see? And infidelity is the least of it, but you have no idea what that does to you."

"That much, I do."

Taylor blinked at him.

He gave a humorless laugh. "Why do you think I called off my engagement a week before the wedding? I walked in on my fiancée with another man."

"I'm sorry."

He shook his head as though to ward off the image. "It's past," he muttered. "The thing is, you take it in stride and you go on."

"It's not that simple, Dev."

"I know it's not, but what else are you going to do? It's worth the fight. Trust me, I know, and it's not just Melissa that taught me that. Everything that went on with my parents, it haunted my sister, and I'm not going to tell you it didn't change me, too, but you can't let stuff like that define the whole direction of your life." He took both her hands in his and stared at her intensely. "They don't deserve that, none of them do. You go on, and you live life on your own terms."

Taylor started to pull away. "I'm through living to other people's expectations, even yours."

"The only expectations you need to meet are your own. I'm just trying to give you another way of thinking about it. If you let it shadow you, then you're still letting him have control." He kissed her fingers. "Just think about what I'm saying. Don't let what happened make you run away from a good thing. I swear, by anything I can think of, that I'll never do anything to hurt you. I swear it.''

THE CHURCH WAS LOVELY AND old, with soaring ceilings and smoothly worn pews. Stained-glass windows filled it with radiance. Shay would have grown up in this church, she guessed, and the white-haired minister who was going to marry him might well have given him his name, long before.

She stared at Dev, standing in his tux by the altar, between Shay and Shay's brother Colin. And Mallory walked down the aisle, looking like a faerie princess in a flowing chiffon gown belted with silk flowers. The organist played Pachelbel's Canon, the notes dancing into the air.

It pulled Taylor back, with an almost physical tug, to her own wedding. She remembered, oh, she remembered walking down that aisle, giddily certain of what she was doing, knowing she'd show everyone. *It will too last*—those words had echoed in her head as she walked. She hadn't even glanced at her mother in the front pew, but walked by with her head held high.

And Bennett, standing up front in his tux with his lord-of-all-he-surveyed expression, he'd made her heart swell with pride that she was the one he'd chosen.

Suddenly everything in her stilled as she sat in the pew, remembering that long ago day. Why hadn't she ever realized it before? It had been so obvious. The seeds of destruction had been sown long before Bennett's abusive side had surfaced. She'd married him for every wrong reason in the world. She'd married him because her parents were against it, she'd married him because she wanted to prove to everyone she could finish something. She'd married him because somehow she'd believed it would make her a grown-up. Deep in her heart of hearts, she'd known there was something wrong, but pride hadn't let her back down, pride and a kind of wild romanticism that wanted to believe in a storybook romance.

Instead she'd gotten a horror story nightmare.

Taylor took in a deep breath of air and watched Mallory and Shay link hands at the altar. Had she and Bennett ever had that sense of equality, that sense of love? She gave her head an almost imperceptible shake, knowing the answer was no, and suddenly not caring.

It was as though she'd been walking around with a heavy load on her shoulders and she'd thrown it off. How was it she'd labored so long in fear? She'd been young, reactive, impulsive. The signs had all been there, she'd simply ignored them. And she'd paid for that, God knew she'd paid, but it wasn't something capricious and mysterious that might catch her un-awares again.

The congregation rose for prayer, and Taylor rose with them. To make the right decisions and live honorably, she thought, sending the thought winging up. That was her prayer. More than that, she couldn't ask for.

A slow grin spread over her face as she saw the groom kiss the bride. Applause broke out. Clasping hands, Mallory and Shay turned around together and walked out as equals, down the aisle and into their future.

And Dev walked past, tossing Taylor a grin and a wink as he escorted Becka out of the church.

Outside, the air was fresh with just the faintest breath of spring. Rebirth, she thought, searching for Dev. A new life.

Taylor walked up and planted a fervent kiss on him.

He blinked. "What was that for?"

"For being generally wonderful."

He leaned toward her. "You think I'm wonderful now, baby, you just wait till tonight."

16

SWINGING A HAMMER USUALLY put him in a good mood, Dev thought as he pounded nails into the studs of a wall designed to divide one of the basement storage rooms. So why did he feel so restless and unsettled? It had been with him from the moment he'd awoken that morning, this sense of somehow not fitting into his life properly, as though he'd put his right shoe on the left foot. He knew it was there; what he couldn't understand was why.

Things were good. The project would finish the following week, on budget and on schedule. Mallory was happy. He and Taylor seemed to have come to an accommodation.

Taylor…

On one hand he felt like they'd talked and made a connection. She'd wanted to run and he'd talked her out of it. On the other hand, it felt like they were in limbo. They had a hot, no hassle affair going. Was there anything wrong with wanting to keep things steady when it worked so well for both of them?

Moodily he slipped his hammer into its loop on his tool belt. Time to go make the rounds and give a call to the building inspector.

The icy rain that dripped down his neck as he walked to the construction trailer didn't improve his frame of mind. He mounted the steps, cursing a little as he opened the door. Then he stepped inside.

And froze, staring at the woman sitting in his chair. She looked like some beauty from a pre-Raphaelite painting, all milk-pale skin, flushed cheeks, and red-gold hair curling down to her waist. She would have been painted as an innocent seduced by a god in the form of a swan, or a naive music student led astray.

"Hello, Dev," she said. In her baggy cream fisherman's sweater, she looked small and vulnerable. He remembered the first time he'd seen her across the room at one of Riley's parties, how his mind had stuttered and stopped at the sight of her, a face imported from across the centuries.

"Melissa." He wrenched his eyes away and turned to the coffeepot. "What are you doing here?"

"I've missed you." Her voice was low and shook a bit. "Have you missed me?"

He concentrated on pouring coffee into the cup. "You know better than to ask that."

"Do I? We don't disconnect from each other as easily as that." She rose to her feet. "You can't just shut me out and pretend that we never existed."

How could she stand there looking so innocent and hurt when she'd betrayed him utterly? Dev felt the weight of the heavy ceramic cup in his hand, wishing he were outside where he could throw it, throw something to burn off the frustration surging through him. "You're acting like you don't remember the last time we saw each other."

Regret shimmered in her eyes. "I wish I could forget it. I wish that you could."

"You think that ignoring it will make it go away?" She'd not only betrayed him, but she'd done it with some cipher, some pretty boy she didn't know from Adam.

"God, Dev, I made a mistake." She raked a hand through her hair and stared at him, her eyes pleading. "I drank too much, I was stupid. I was just thinking about how it was my last chance to get crazy and spontaneous."

"Well, now, see, it wasn't, as it turns out," he said conversationally. "You're free to be as crazy and spontaneous as you want anytime you want."

"And all I want is you," she said, tears shimmering in her eyes.

Dev tightened his jaw. Don't buy into this, he told himself. Don't let her sell you. Every time they'd had a fight, it had gone this way. Every time they'd had a fight—and they'd had them often—she'd come to him contrite, sorrowful, telling him how much he meant to her, telling him that she'd change. And once she'd convinced him, once she'd manipulated him into doing what she wanted, she'd turn back into the self-absorbed person she truly was.

"We're no good together, Melissa," he said, reminding himself as much as her.

She stared at him, and a confidence bordering on arrogance flickered in her eyes. "I don't believe that. We fit."

"No."

"You wanted me then and you still want me now."

"We have different goals. Even before the Jack and Jill party, we fought all the time." Even to his own ears he didn't sound convinced.

"All that means is that we're two different people, both very passionate about what we believe," she said softly. "That makes us human, and humans make mistakes. That's what this breakup is all about, a mistake.''

"You really believe that?"

"Yes, I do. And so do you."

TAYLOR SAT IN HER OFFICE staring at her computer screen. She shook her head and for the hundredth time dragged her thoughts away from Dev and on to the work at hand. The problem was, they didn't want to stay there. Things had changed for her over the weekend, perhaps they'd been changing all along, but they were definitely different now and she needed to decide what to do about it.

One thing was incontestable—she loved him. No matter how panicky it had made her, it was her reality. She took a deep breath and made herself face the idea. It wasn't necessarily a bad thing. Dev Carson was not Bennett, she reminded herself. He was someone she liked, someone she respected; someone who understood her, he'd demonstrated that the night before. Time and again, he'd showed her he cared for her, he'd filled her life with fun, light, passion, and the unexpected. The wonder wasn't that she loved him, it was that it had taken her so long to realize it.

To tell him or not, that was the question. And if she decided to tell him, how did she do it? Just how did you break news like that to a man, she mused. With Bennett, she'd been too young to really understand what she was saying, and he'd said it to her first, anyway. But how to tell a man so that he understood it was a gift, not an obligation, so that he didn't feel trapped or pressured to say it in return? She shook her head. That much was a mystery.

Have him over to her apartment and cook a romantic dinner? Too fraught with expectation. Tell him in bed one night, after they'd finished making love? Too clichéd, she decided. Send him a note? Too wimpy.

She gave a growl of frustration. Maybe she should just keep it to herself. Certainly it would be safer, but she was through with playing life safe. It was time to take chances.

The light on her phone flashed and Taylor picked the handset up.

"Mr. Champlin of Champlin Travel is here to see you."

DEV LOOKED AT MELISSA and tried to ignore the pounding in his temples.

"In a way, I think this breakup has been good for us," she said, walking over to the trailer door. "It's shown us both just what we mean to each other." Eyes bright, gaze bold, she locked it and turned back to him.

"Well, that's the problem, isn't it? I thought we already knew what we meant to each other back when we got engaged. I guess I was wrong."

"No. You do mean something to me, Dev, you do." Melissa moved closer to him. "But till death do us part is a long time. It made me panic. I mean, you're a man. You understand what it's like to feel like you're about to be tied forever."

He thought of the luminous look on Mallory's face as she'd made her vows. "I thought that was the point."

"Oh, come off it." Her temper flared for an instant before she banked it back. "Don't tell me that you didn't at least think about having one last fling before we married.''

"I didn't. I thought about you.''

"Exactly.'' She stared at him and the contrition slid into arrogance. "You're not happy, Dev, it shows all over you. You're missing something.'' She flowed up against him, sliding her arms around his neck. "And that something is me.''

STEPPING TO HER OFFICE DOOR, Taylor watched Champlin walk down the room, across the lush, royal-blue carpet. With his graying beard and his tortoise-shell glasses, he looked more like a college English professor than a businessman. "Good morning, Alan,'' she said, watching his bemused air turn into a smile.

"I was admiring your new digs,'' he said, giving her hand a brisk shake. "Boy, they really did this place from the ground up.''

"Pretty much. I'm glad I've got the long-term lease. I'm sure someone's getting soaked to pay for all the renovation.'' She turned back to her office and gestured for him to follow. "Have a seat.'' She waited for him to sit in her client chair before she dropped in her own chair.

"Let's cut to the chase,'' he said, giving her a direct look, all traces of the college professor evaporating. "I want a merger and I want you on my team. I've got a package that I think will make that happen.''

Taylor picked up a pen and ran it restlessly through her fingers. "Alan, we've been through this. I don't want to sell out. Let's not waste your time.''

"I don't think it's a waste. I've got fifteen stores in the mid-Atlantic, mostly in mall locations."

"You mostly go after the vacation trade."

He nodded. "We've been doing well, but I'd like to see us do better."

"I'm not willing to be swallowed up just so you can get some prime office space." She started to rise.

"It's not about office space," he said quickly. "I want to start a corporate travel division of Champlin and I want you to run it."

Taylor froze and then slowly she sat back down. "You've got my attention. Go on."

He smiled faintly. "I've been watching you scooping up the corporate clients."

"That's interesting." A hint of frost entered her voice. "And just how have you managed that? Do you have a spy in my office?"

"No, I've just been on the receiving end of the thanks but no thanks phone calls from the clients." He gave a thin smile. "Chasing your dust is not amusing."

"What makes you think I can have the same track record working in your organization? In my agency, I've got the freedom to cut whatever deals I want and provide the services that will tip the clients into signing."

Champlin didn't blink. "You'll have the same freedom if you come on board with us. It'll be a separate division headquartered out of this office. You'll be executive vice president and have a seat on the board."

"What's in it for you?"

"Revenue," he said simply. "You'll have complete authority to run it as you see fit, I'm not about to mess with your magic.''

"The financial package..."

"Will be quite generous, both for the buyout and for your salary." He opened his attaché case and pulled out a folder. "This hits the highlights, I believe."

Taylor scanned the sheet and laid her hand on the desk in an effort to keep it from shaking. "I'm not prepared to make a decision today."

"I'd think less of you if you were."

"One other thing. I'm planning to go back to school in the fall." The words were out before she knew she was going to say them. "If we do come to an agreement, it will need to include some provision for that."

"Great. Go nights and we'll cover your tuition if you agree to stick around at least a couple of years after you graduate. An investment in your education is an investment in the company. So am I correct in thinking you're willing to consider my proposal?"

Taylor took her time in answering. One thing she'd learned in her business was negotiation. "I'd certainly like to review it. I can't say more than that until I've spoken with my lawyer."

"Fair enough. I'll give you a couple of days."

"A week," she said firmly. "You're asking me to sell out a business that I've devoted years to building."

"So that you can build something bigger." He waited for a beat. "All right, a week. I'll look forward to your response."

The bubble of excitement rose into her throat as they stood and she walked him out. This could be the professional opportunity she'd been waiting for. Suddenly everything looked different. Not even the drizzle outside could dampen her mood as she shook hands with him and watched him walk out the door. If anything, the bubble became bigger.

She had to tell someone or she was going to burst. Not the other agents; it was too preliminary for that. Her body had her heading out the door before her mind caught up with the obvious: find Dev and tell him.

The chill drizzle misted her hair as she walked out to the pedestrian tunnel and around the corner to the construction trailer. This was the pleasure of being involved, she thought. Not just the wild sex and the laughter. It was sharing triumphs and joys.

Taylor turned the handle of the door on the construction trailer. When it clicked and held solid, she blinked in surprise. The trailer usually remained open during business hours, but perhaps Dev was meeting with an inspector and didn't want to be disturbed.

It didn't matter, Taylor told herself, pushing down her disappointment. The evening was soon enough. Over dinner and a glass of wine, she'd tell him about Champlin's offer, and she'd tell him what was in her heart.

She'd tell him she loved him.

17

LIFE WAS FULL OF SURPRISES, Dev thought later that evening as he unlocked his front door. The road was never straight. Every time he thought he knew where he was going, it veered without warning. When he'd woken that morning, the world as he'd known it had looked one way. Now, in a heartbeat, it had changed completely.

He took off his coat and hung it over a hook on the hall tree. The lingering hint of Melissa's perfume clung to his shirt, reminding him of what he had learned and what he had lost. Without the right woman, a man was nowhere, he thought. Without the woman he loved. How could he have not realized what she meant to him? And what was he supposed to do about it now?

He crossed into the dining room where he'd temporarily exiled his refrigerator. He leaned on the open door and studied the contents, but what he was really seeing was—

The knock on the door made him jump. "Dev?" Taylor's voice called.

Taylor, he thought, and immediately he remembered the perfume. In his own time and place, he'd tell her what had happened. Maybe it would upset her, maybe she wouldn't understand when he told her what he'd learned about himself, but she'd accept it, he thought. Whereas if she smelled another woman on him, he was pretty sure the conversation would begin and end right there.

"It's open," he called, vaulting up the stairs, unbuttoning his shirt as he ran.

"Where are you?" she said from the entryway.

"Get yourself a drink," he called. "I'm taking a shower." He tore at the laces on his boots and kicked them off; his shirt and jeans landed on the carpet. Even as he turned on the taps in the shower, he heard the front door shut.

He jumped into the stall while the water was still icy.

"Sweetheart, are you upstairs?"

"In the shower," he said, trying not to curse as the cold water sluiced through his hair. It wasn't nearly as cold as Taylor would be when she found out about Melissa. He'd tell her—he couldn't hold it back—but in his own way and in his own time.

TAYLOR PULLED OFF HER GLOVES and hung up her coat. One of the small annoyances of winter was having to go everywhere piled with clothing. Oh, for the sultry air of Mexico.

Water from upstairs rushed through the pipes in the walls. She climbed up the staircase, her hand sliding on the satiny oak baluster. The house was such a strange mix of restored, run-down and work in progress. The kitchen, she imagined, was still a confusion of plaster dust and torn out bits of lath. Here in the entryway, though, she could have walked back in time to the year the house had first been built.

How could she not love a man who would put such focus, such pride into bringing back part of the past?

She thought of him showing her the photographs of the house in its heyday. Other men might renovate because it was a good investment. Dev was doing it because he loved the house and its history, because bringing beauty back to life satisfied him. And knowing all that only made her adore him all the more.

So when, she wondered. Tell him now, before they did anything? Lure him out to dinner somewhere romantic and tell him? Wait until evening, when they could sit in front of the fire? It seemed both momentous and liberating, a feeling within her that was crying out to be said.

She'd know when the time was right, Taylor decided as she turned into his bedroom and saw the steam drifting out of the bathroom. A smile played about her lips as she began unbuttoning her shirt. For now, she'd just go keep Dev company and leave the rest to fate.

Though the other parts of the house were chilly, the bathroom was warm and damp with steam. Even the mahogany floor was cozy against her feet. Shower curtains hanging from a metal ring shrouded the claw-foot tub. "Can you spare a cup of water, neighbor?" Taylor slipped her hands in the seam where the curtains met and stepped in.

Dev pulled her against him.

"Mmm. Naked, wet. We need to start meeting like this more often."

Giddy joy surged through her. This man, this beautiful, wonderful man, was her lover, her love. The stream of water had stripped his hair back from his face, letting her admire the carved out cheekbones, the taut line of the jaw, that enticing cleft in his chin, and his eyes, deep set, glowing green, casting their spell on her.

"And do you need to clean up after a hard day's work?" he murmured, leaning close to her.

"Well, if you can spare a little soap."

Slick with suds, his hands slid over her body, running over her breasts until her nipples swelled. "I don't know," he said, holding up his dwindling soap on a rope. "There isn't too much here. Maybe we should reuse it." He pulled her against him and slid up and down her body. She could feel him stiffening against her.

"I'm all for recycling," she said breathlessly, then gasped as his slippery fingers trailed down her hip and up her thighs to unerringly find that place where she didn't need soap or water to be wet, slick and achingly sensitive.

Dev turned her back into the hot stream of water so that it sluiced over her shoulders and back. Taylor groped for the soap, but it slipped through her fingers before she could get a grip on it, tumbling onto the bottom of the tub.

"I'll get it," Dev said and crouched down, reaching through her legs and behind her even as he kissed her thighs. Taylor felt the warmth of his lips move up as his fingers traced the back of her calves, then spiraled higher, the soap in his hand making a tantalizing trail. She shivered at the feel of his tongue licking at the indentation where her thigh met her flat belly. For a whirling moment, he nuzzled at her, pressing her legs apart as she struggled for balance, clutching at his shoulders.

Then his mouth was hot against her, his tongue slipping into the folds and creases to find the swollen bud that was at the center of the tension that had her strung tight as a wire. The first stroke sent her jolting and gasping against him. The second stroke made her moan. And then it was simply a vortex that immersed her in a dark seduction where emotion and sensation catalyzed into something far greater. He'd taken her before to places she'd never been to physically, but this blazing desire roaring through her was something more.

It wasn't slow and gradual. It wasn't gentle. It flung her over the edge and into freefall, giddy, spiraling down for an endless time.

Dev rose and pulled her against him.

"I don't think I can stand," she murmured.

"Sure you can stand. You're not entirely clean yet," he said, running the soap over her body, resensitizing it. "We need to get you lathered up some more."

"Uh-uh, my turn." Taylor reached out for the egg of soap, working it in her hands until it lathered. "You can do interesting things with a soap this size," she said teasingly, feeling his erection nudge against her belly, heavy and hard. Then she ran the soap down the underside of his cock, running it up and down until he groaned.

Feeling her move against him while she was in the throes of orgasm had had him nearly coming himself. Now, with her body slick and warm under his hands and the teasing touch of the soap running against the sensitive skin, he fought to hold himself back. He wanted to feel her around him, tight and hot, for a long, long time before he let himself go over.

Dev turned her away from the water so that she would be focused only on his touch, and gently pried away the soap. He wanted more even as he wanted to pull back from the edge. Running the soap over her breast, he circled the nipple. He focused on it, trying to concentrate on something besides the way her fingers on his cock sent tremors of desire through him with each stroke. He moved the soap lower, sliding it over her hips, the cheeks of her ass, along her thighs, then slipping it up between them.

He heard Taylor catch her breath as he brushed the soap between her hidden lips, stroking it over her clit until he felt her tremble and clutch at his shoulders. "It's important to be clean all over," he murmured in her ear.

The silky soft touch brought the barest friction to her but it was enough to have her shivering, all her nerve endings, all the passion reignited.

Taylor jolted as she felt his fingers slipping into her. "More," she muttered into his ear, moving against him, her hand moving steadily up and down on him. "I want you inside me. Fill me up."

"Don't be so impatient," he said and she shivered at the brush of the soap against her clit again, against those sensitive folds that surrounded it. "I want to get you nice and slippery and ready."

"Now," she whispered against his neck. She made a little sound of satisfaction as she felt him press her legs apart. Then she gasped as he slid the soap up inside her instead.

There was something deliciously different about having that feeling of solid fullness in her even as she held his cock in her hands. The soap was solid and slick as he slid it out of her and across her clit, then back in, stroking across excruciatingly responsive nerve endings until she cried out. His soapy fingers slid down her back and over her buttocks, caressing them and slipping into the cleft in between, touching the fragile, sensitive spot there that sent shocks through her system.

It was too overwhelming, too much pleasure coming from too many places at once. Taylor cried out in no known language, on the edge of going over.

"I have to be in you," he muttered, dropping the soap and turning her so that her back was against the wall.

And it was as though everything that had come before was just a game, child's play compared to what rocked through her when she helped Dev slide himself up inside her. When she cried out, her voice blended with his. When she shuddered, the movement began in her body and ended in his. And when he began to move, the flow of desire surged between them.

She clutched at his shoulders. He pulled her to him and buried his face in her neck. And when the orgasm hit, she had no way of telling in whose body it began and in whose body it ended. It was the two of them together.

MAKING IT TO HIS BED was as far as they could manage. Clothing would have to wait. Taylor lay with one leg draped between Dev's, leaning her arms on his chest. "We got your sheets all wet."

"I didn't think I could stand up long enough to find a towel."

"I've been doing some thinking," she began, touching her fingertip to a bead of water on his neck and spreading it into a circle.

"So have I."

"What about?"

He smiled faintly. "Ladies first."

Taylor stared into the green of his eyes, trying to dive into the depths, willing him to connect with her. "I've never had anything like the time I spent with you in Mexico. It was really special. Part of it was that it was a gorgeous resort, but most of it was due to you. It wouldn't have been nearly as great if you hadn't been there." She stopped. Clumsy, clumsy, clumsy. Why couldn't she get it out? She'd thought about it for two days, she was absolutely certain of how she felt, and he needed to know it. All she had to do was say those three words. She'd said them before, after all.

But this would be the first time she'd ever said them and really meant them.

Dev stroked a hand over her hair. "It was special for me, too," he said.

"There's something you ought to know," she began again. "Something I need to tell you. I—"

The phone shrilled in the silence and Taylor's words died in her throat. Dev made no move to get it.

"Don't you want to answer that?"

"I'm more interested in hearing what you have to say. Besides, it's probably a telemarketer or something." He brushed her hair back gently from her face and raised his head to kiss her. "Talk to me."

But the noise of the ring had her rattled, and the brief surge of courage had deserted her. She began again, dragging together the backbone to tell him the way she felt, to lay it out for him to do as he would.

Across the room, on the highboy, the answering machine beeped, then a woman's sultry voice poured into the room. "Hi gorgeous, are you there? It's me. Melissa."

18

HE TENSED.

Even through the sudden turmoil in her head, Taylor registered first and foremost the rigidity of his muscles, the taut, pared down expression on his face.

Ice arrowed through her.

"It was so good to see you today," Melissa purred over the answering machine speaker. "I know it was stupid of me to start things in the trailer, but I couldn't help it. It's been so long, for both of us, and you felt so good." She gave a sultry chuckle. "Besides, you know how I've always loved nooners with you. And I locked the door."

Never in her life had Taylor felt so naked as now, draped against Dev's nude body while the voice of his ex-fiancée—his lover?—came through the phone. The hackles rose on the back of her neck. She moved to rise, but he tightened his arm to hold her against him.

"You've got to know how much I love you, Dev. And I know how you feel about me. God, it was so good to have you hold me again. I think today showed us both we need to give it another try. Call me." She disconnected.

Taylor shoved, pulled, scratched to get loose from him and rose quickly to sit on the edge of the bed.

"Taylor." Dev caught at her arm, but she shook him off.

Instead she rose to her feet and walked to the chair where she'd left her clothing earlier, slipping into her lingerie. The thing to do was get dressed and get out. Don't think, she told herself, just dress. Stay calm. Don't feel this vicious, impossible pain.

"It's not what you think."

Her calm shuddered a little at Dev's voice. She ignored him and stepped into her trousers. The floor creaked, and then he was behind her, his hands on her shoulders.

And calm shattered all to pieces.

She whirled and jerked away. "I was at your trailer today at lunch. The door was locked." She hadn't thought she could feel anything more but when he closed his eyes, betrayal sliced through her.

"Taylor, nothing happened."

"Really?" Her voice cracked. "It sure didn't sound that way listening to her talk." She searched for her socks, rescuing them from the corner.

"Look, I didn't agree to meet her. I walked into the trailer and she was just there. But we didn't do anything."

"She seems to think you did."

"And she's wrong, as usual. Look, what do you want me to say?"

She glared at him. "I want you to tell me you didn't have your arms around your fiancée."

Dev looked at her for a moment in silence, then looked away.

"Right," Taylor said, buttoning her shirt.

Dev dragged on his jeans and sat on the edge of the bed. "Look," he said, reaching toward her.

Taylor jerked back. "Just tell me what happened," she said. "All of it."

His jaw tightened. "Melissa's been calling me ever since I went to Mexico. And I haven't returned one call. I haven't wanted to," he said emphatically.

"Then how do you explain that?" she replied, gesturing to the answering machine.

"I went to the trailer today at lunch and she was there, waiting for me. I guess Riley must have let her in."

"Riley?" Taylor said blankly. "What does he have to do with this?"

Dev shook his head wearily. "He's her cousin. We met at one of his parties. His mother's been on him about Melissa and me because no one else besides Riley knows why we broke up."

"Fine. Then what?"

"She said she wanted to talk. She apologized, said she'd been foolish and regretted it, but that she still loved me. We belonged together, she said, she still wanted me. And then she locked the door."

"And let me guess, you screamed for the police," she said sarcastically, jamming her feet into her boots and zipping them up. She was strong enough to get through this, she told herself fiercely. It wasn't going to flatten her this time. She'd hear him out, see what kind of person he was.

And then she'd walk away and never look back.

Dev dragged his fingers through his hair. "Everything since the Jack and Jill party has just been such a blur. I've been so caught up in it—finding her with that guy, going to Mexico, being with you, the craziness back here. It's all happened too fast." He raised his head and looked at her, eyes intense. "I haven't been taking time to think, and that's been a mistake. That's how people get hurt. When I was in the trailer with Melissa and she put her arms around me, I realized that—''

The phone rang again. Both of them stared at it until the answering machine clicked and Melissa's voice came out again. "Dev, honey, pick up the phone, I know you're there. I can't stop thinking about you, I can't stop thinking about touching you. I need to see you. I love you," she whispered, and hung up.

Taylor stared at him, shaking her head. "I've been through this, God, I've been through this. I thought it was different this time but it's just the same."

"Taylor, nothing happened," Dev burst out.

The words shivered in the silence of the room.

She stood up slowly. "You know, you were in an awful hurry to get into the shower today. You usually let me in and kiss me hello, you don't just bolt. It seemed weird at the time, but now maybe it's not so odd after all." She glanced at his shirt, then did a double-take and lifted it off the floor by one fingertip and examined the collar. "Estée Lauder cocoa plum? Nice shade of lipstick," she said cuttingly.

"You're jumping to conclusions."

She gave a humorless laugh. "Do you blame me? Your fiancée—"

"Ex-fiancée."

"Whatever," she said impatiently. "She calls and talks about touching you and wanting you, her smell and her lipstick is all over your shirt, you bolt to the shower, your trailer was locked. What am I supposed to think?"

"Maybe you could trust me," he said quietly, staring at her.

"This isn't the first time that I've found the man I love playing around with someone else."

Dev's eyes widened at her words, but she didn't notice.

"Oh, yeah, I'm getting practice. And I'm getting better at walking away all the time," Taylor said grimly. She wanted to rage, to weep. And finally, she just wanted it over. "You know what, it's irrelevant whether you did anything or not. What matters is that you still have feelings for her. If you hadn't, you'd have told me about it."

"It didn't mean anything," he repeated.

She studied him for a moment. "Are you sure about that? Can you honestly tell me you didn't have any feelings for her in that trailer, that you weren't at least tempted?" She shook her head. "If you wanted out, Dev, all you had to do was say so. You didn't have to put me through this."

"I don't want out."

"Well, guess what?" Her eyes flashed. "I do."

DEV SAT ON THE BED and methodically ran through every curse word he knew. Then he started at the beginning and ran through it all again. Finally he stood up and pulled a shirt on, laced on his work boots. Talking would only tempt him to shout, and thinking would only make him crazy. He knew what he needed to do.

Ten minutes later, he was in what was technically speaking his kitchen, swinging a hammer, losing himself in the controlled violence of pounding nails. Steadily, methodically, he built the studs for the new interior walls, lattices of parallel two-by-fours with top and bottom crown pieces. He focused on the wood and on the job at hand, consciously avoiding thinking about the day he and Taylor had torn down the walls.

Torn down his walls, shown him what life could be like.

Sound exploded as Dev slammed 2-inch nails into two-by-fours with such violence that a single blow sank them completely. Over and over, with a numbing repetition, he reached for a nail, grabbed a slab of wood, and created order and structure by the force of his mind and his body. He took grim pleasure in wrestling warped pieces into position, nailing in a temporary fulcrum and muscling them straight, then holding them, arms trembling, until he could slam them in place with nails.

When his muscles began to ache, he welcomed it. When sweat began dripping, he stripped his shirt off and went onward. He wouldn't have been able to guess at the passing time; his goal was not to know.

The pounding at his front door had been going on for long minutes before he registered it. Finally he tossed down his hammer, the metal ringing on the bare concrete of the room. With a glance at the clock, he went to face the person at the door, doubtlessly a neighbor complaining about the noise.

It wasn't.

"Jesus, Dev, I've been out here for five minutes. What the hell are you doing?" Riley stood on the porch, face pinched with cold.

Dev turned without a word and walked back into the house.

Riley followed in his wake. "Look, I bet you're kind of mad at me."

"What would make you think that?" Dev bit off the words without turning as he walked down the central hall to his kitchen.

Riley stepped into the room and paced around restlessly. "Man, you've been going to town in here. I didn't think you were going to start this for a couple of weeks."

"The schedule changed."

"You doing tip up studs or building it piecemeal?"

Dev stopped and looked at him. "Riley, what are you doing here? I'm not in the mood for company, particularly not yours. What do you want?"

Riley shifted uneasily. "I, uh, wanted to see how you were doing. I mean, Melissa called me tonight."

Dev looked at him coldly. "And you're here to check it out?"

"No." Riley stood foursquare. "Look, I told her where to find you, I'll admit that. But I'm not her weasel. I came here to see what was up with you."

"Well, as you can see, I'm busy." Dev picked up the end of a two-by-four.

Riley grabbed the other end and helped Dev align it to the crown piece. "Come on, Dev, don't be ticked with me."

Dev picked up his hammer and put a pair of nails between his lips, holding them by the tips. "You think I'm ticked?" he grunted, pounding the hammer down on a nail in a powerful swing. "I'll clue you in, buddy. This isn't ticked." He sank the nail with a second hit. "This is what we call ripshit." He slammed the second nail, sinking it in a single stroke, and raised his head to look at Riley furiously. "Thanks to you and your helpfulness, everything is completely, totally, and utterly ruined."

Riley looked chastened as he brought over another two-by-four. "I just thought—"

"No." Dev cut him off. "That's the trouble, you didn't think. Melissa—or your mama—sold you on her little song and dance and you did what she wanted. She's great at making herself look like the victim when it suits her purposes, and great at screwing everything up when it doesn't. She lies, she manipulates to get what she wants. And you should know it by now."

He stopped, abruptly spent, and sat down.

"So you told her things were finished, right?" Riley asked. "That means it's done."

Dev shook his head wearily. "Yeah, it's done all right. And it's looking like that's not all. Taylor was here tonight when Melissa called to give me one of her little performances on the answering machine. Before I'd had a chance to tell Taylor about it."

Riley gave a low whistle.

Dev nodded. "Melissa was in rare form. She spun it out so it sounded like we'd dropped in the trailer and gone at it."

"So Taylor's pissed, I take it."

"No, Taylor's gone."

Riley blinked. "Well, just go and explain it to her."

"I tried to explain it to her." Dev rose and reached for another nail and his hammer. "She didn't want to hear it. When you've gotten a divorce because you walked in on your husband with another woman, you're kind of reluctant to cut the next guy much slack."

"Oh. But you didn't actually do Melissa, though." Riley paused. "Did you?" Dev shot him a killing glare. "Right, so it's not really a crisis. All you have to do is let Taylor cool down and tell her what really happened."

"Why is she going to listen later when she wouldn't listen now?"

"I don't know, maybe she'll miss you." He gave a half smile that Dev ignored. "Look, I'll vouch for you."

Dev gave him a cold look and slammed home another nail, then dropped the hammer to the floor. He shook his head and put his hands on his hips, staring down at the concrete. "Goddamn it," he said under his breath.

Riley stood for a moment and stared at the same patch of floor as if he might see whatever Dev's imagination was conjuring there. Then he coughed and stepped to Dev's side. "So how did you leave it?"

"You know, I realized something when I was talking with Melissa today," Dev said, ignoring the question. "I've been paying attention to every other damned thing in the world other than what really matters."

"What does that mean? What really matters? Are you in love with Melissa?"

"No." Dev kicked the hammer and sent it skittering across the floor. "I'm in love with Taylor."

19

EARLY AFTERNOON SUN spilled through the front windows of the travel agency, without, for the first time in five months, being blocked by scaffolding. It should have made Taylor feel good that the construction was finally finished.

It didn't.

It would have taken more than just sunlight to brighten her outlook. It would have taken temporary amnesia, a very specific amnesia that left her with no memory of Dev Carson outside of the first time she'd seen him. To have the peace of mind that that would engender, she'd give up Pace-Miller, she'd give up Champlin's job offer. In exchange for wiping Dev Carson from her mind, she'd give up almost anything.

Unfortunately no one was offering, and short of clonking herself in the head with a brick on the off chance of success, it looked like she'd just have to live with it.

And live with it, she would, she told herself fiercely. After all, it wasn't as though she hadn't been through infidelity before. She'd been through it and survived. She'd survived Bennett, she'd survived the divorce, and she'd come back stronger than ever. Then again, getting over Bennett had been like getting over an illness. Getting over Dev felt more like getting past an amputation of a limb, the knowledge that some vital part of her was now gone forever.

The loss was bitter, the betrayal raw and deep. It was unbearable.

She had to find a way to bear it.

Taylor put her fingertips against her eyes, pressing until rainbow patterns appeared behind her closed lids. She had to forget. She had to get past it. It was pointless to think about him, so she told herself every time she thought about him.

It had gotten to where she was telling herself that all the time, because that was how often she thought of him. And why? He wasn't worth it, she told herself. He wasn't the man he'd appeared to be. He wasn't the man she loved.

So why was it she couldn't stop thinking about him? And wondering if he really had been telling her the truth.

Nicole knocked on the door and Taylor jumped. "Sorry, didn't mean to scare you. I picked up your pictures." Nicole tossed the red and white drugstore bag on Taylor's desk.

Dimly she remembered asking Nicole to pick up her developed film, when she found out she was going to the drugstore. "How much was it?" Taylor asked, fumbling for her purse.

Nicole shrugged. "I don't know. I got some other stuff. The receipt's in the bag."

Taylor opened up the film envelope and spilled the glossy stack of images into her hand.

Nicole moved to look over her shoulder and whistled. "Nice. Where's that?"

"Barbados," Taylor murmured. Lush and tropical,

it would be perfect for the photo album she kept to show prospective customers who needed convincing.

"And that?"

"St. Thomas."

Sun and sand, white stucco buildings with brightly painted doors and shutters. Palm trees, aqua ocean.

Dev.

The thought of him was inextricably tied to the hot climates, but Taylor struggled to shrug it off. She had to get used to not thinking about him, because it wasn't going to get any better otherwise.

The front door jingled, and Nicole straightened up. "I'd better get out there. Glynnis left for lunch when I came in. Don't put those away, though. I want to finish looking at them later."

"Sure."

Nicole paused in the doorway. "You know, if you ever need to send me down there to check out properties and collect photos, I'll be happy to do it. Just in case you were wondering. I could use a vacation. You know, a hot spot, a hot guy…"

"Be careful what you ask for," Taylor murmured.

"Or you will surely get it? Baby, that's what I'm counting on," Nicole laughed as she turned away.

Absently Taylor flipped through the rest of the stack, a record of two weeks of island hopping. St. Croix, Antigua, St. Lucia. Sultry days, sultry nights, the memories came streaming back as she shuffled through the pictures.

And then she froze. In her hand, glossy and golden, was a smiling photo of her with Dev. They were wrapped together and laughing, the background a lush fantasy of luxuriant palms, vines, and blossoms.

Some part of her mind railed that she was being

foolish to stare at something that was done and over. She should enjoy the momentary memory of pleasure and move on. Accept that he wasn't the one for her. They'd said no strings; the fact that he'd taken a more liberal translation of it was just her bad luck. And even if he hadn't, he must still have feelings for Melissa or he'd have said something.

Enough, she told herself. It made no sense for pain to gouge her like this. But then feelings had never had much to do with sense anyway. It would get easier, she reminded herself. She had simply gotten used to Dev, that was all. As she became accustomed to his absence, the pain would fade. It had to.

Didn't it?

She stared at the photo, looking into Dev's eyes as though she could bring him to life as she'd known him then, before that night, before that call.

Before it all changed.

She'd get used to it, Taylor told herself again. Instead, to her horror, tears pricked at the back of her eyelids.

She rose and hurried toward the bathroom, blinking.

"You okay, Taylor?" Nicole asked as she walked by.

"Something in my eye." Whether it was convincing or not didn't really concern Taylor. Once she got to the small, dark room and closed the door, she could let go of control for just a few seconds. The way she'd done for hours every night for the past week.

The way she was afraid she was going to do for a very long time.

IT WAS DONE. FINISHED. At an end, and good rid-
dance to it.

Dev sat at his desk, reviewing the final report on
the renovations. He still needed to get a final release
from the landlord, he thought, staring at the form on
his computer screen, but after five months, the job
was over.

And that was probably for the best, he thought.
Definitely. Sure, it meant that he'd no longer be working around Taylor, but given that she wanted nothing
to do with him, that was sort of a good thing.

Certainly it would keep him from the temptation of
digging up reasons to stop by and see her, or hang
around outside of her agency on the chance of running into her.

Of course, it made sense to get her to formally signoff on her unit. So much had gone wrong there that
it could only help to get a release saying that everything was all set.

It was the smart thing to do, he told himself as he
typed in a few quick edits and sent the file to the
printer.

The agency looked good, he thought a few minutes
later when he walked in. With the carpet and light
fixtures in place as the finishing touches, it looked
sleek, professional and expensive. He'd become
enough of a regular that the receptionist merely
waved at him as he walked back toward Taylor's office. Yep, get in, get business done, and get out. Now
was not the time to get caught up in longing for something that wasn't going to work out.

He stepped into Taylor's doorway, his hand raised
to knock, and paused. Her chair was empty. Probably
just as well. He could lay the paperwork on her desk,

add a note telling her what to do with it, and head out.

He walked to her desk and pulled a pen out of his back pocket. All he needed was a yellow sticky note, he thought, looking around. Then he saw the photo, and in a flicker, he was back in Cozumel, pulling her against him as they smiled for Raoul. What was it doing there? Why hadn't she tossed it out? He shook his head, hard, to dislodge the image.

If he'd learned nothing else from his time with Melissa it was knowing when to give up.

And then he saw the shell.

TAYLOR WALKED BACK INTO HER office to a flashing phone. She dropped into her chair, trying to ignore the throbbing in her temples, and lifted the handset.

"Taylor DeWitt."

"Taylor. Alan Champlin. How are you doing?"

She mustered up a smile. "I'm fine, thanks." Perhaps if she said it enough times, she might actually come to believe it. "How are you?"

"Great, or I will be if I get the right answer from you. Did you have a chance to look at the paperwork?"

The merger, she remembered. The job offer. Her lawyer had given her the thumbs-up on it and she was ready to agree, with a few minor revisions. She reached across her desk for the file and saw an unfamiliar sheet of paper bearing the logo for Dev's company. Which meant that someone from the company had been in her office.

Dev?

"Taylor, you there?" Champlin asked.

"I'm here, Alan. I'm just looking for the file." She

rescued the folder and turned to the paperwork. "Well, it made my lawyer and my accountant happy, so we're halfway there."

"The key is, did it make *you* happy?"

As if anything could at this point in time. With an almost physical effort, she dragged her mind away from Dev and back to the subject at hand. "There are a couple of minor points about transfer of assets that I'd like to close on, and I'd like to get the tuition reimbursement written into my contract, but if we can come to an agreement on those, then yes, the deal looks good."

"Excellent," Champlin said. "Welcome to the team."

And even as dark as she felt, the little pump of excitement was there, nudging at her, reminding her that her world would go on without Dev Carson.

But would it ever be complete?

SITTING IN A CROUCH, Dev maneuvered a sheet of drywall against the new studs of his kitchen and propped it into position using a prybar and the fingers of one hand. He used the other hand to sink a couple of screws in to hold it in place. Bless the inventor of magnetic drill bits, he thought as he strained to hold the heavy paper-sheathed plaster for another moment until it was pinned against the two-by-fours. Then he rose and began sinking screws every six inches, smoothly and methodically as an automaton.

If only he could keep his brain as empty as an automaton's. Unfortunately it kept running back to the subject of Taylor. What did it mean that their photo was on her desk? What did it mean that she'd kept the shell he'd given her in Cozumel? He could go to her and convince her to try again, he knew, but what would it matter if she was still caught up in the past? He'd just be laboring against the same issues.

Wasn't that what he'd done with Melissa? He pushed another panel of Sheetrock up against the studs and tacked it. He'd kept at the relationship bloody-mindedly because he didn't want to walk away and wonder if he could have made it work if he'd just tried a little harder. Over and over he'd convinced himself he could do it. Over and over he'd come back to it, long after he should have been gone.

What if Taylor were another version of the same thing?

Dev put the final screw in the drywall panel and looked around the room. It was ready for taping and mudding. After that, it would need ceiling texture, moldings, paint, and that was just the beginning. It was hard work, he thought, rubbing at his trapezius muscles, and yet ultimately it would be its own reward. In the end, he'd walk into an impeccably restored kitchen and know that he'd done it. And it might take a month or two to finish it, but it would mean more than if he'd hired a crew to come do it in a week. It would be worth it.

In the same way, he couldn't help but wonder if Taylor would be worth it. Sure, he'd been wrong about Melissa and it had left a bad taste in his mouth, but some part of him was convinced that despite all the reasons he had to walk away from Taylor, he'd be a fool to do it.

He remembered too well what it was like to be with her. Yes, she was far from easy. But being with her was like finding a lost part of himself, a part he had never known was missing.

Then again, what if he was just kidding himself, like a gambler who kept going back to the table in search of the ultimate score? He could drive himself crazy by flipping back and forth like some uncertain teenager. Indecision was for children, and Dev had lost his childhood long ago.

He looked at the half-finished walls of the kitchen, the exposed framing of the new wall, the Sheetrock that he had attached with his own hands. He remembered the sweat that had gone into it. Things that were worthwhile took effort, he thought suddenly. Tearing things down was easy. It was the building that took sweat and dedication.

And suddenly he knew what to do.

TAYLOR SAT AT HER DESK, staring at paperwork. Staring at the photo of herself with Dev that she'd propped up against her stapler. It was ridiculous to keep it, she knew. Tearing it up and tossing it into the trash would be the smartest thing she could do. As long as she was looking at him, she'd never get him out of her head.

And she'd never get the thought out of her head that maybe nothing really had happened with his fiancée.

Taylor slapped her pen down on the desk in frustration. That was the worst part, the fact that she couldn't entirely extinguish the hope, the wishful thinking, the vain idea that perhaps he really had cared for her. That he'd wanted her.

That he'd loved her.

But that was just a fantasy. The scaffolding was gone and that morning she'd seen them bring in a truck to haul away the construction trailer. Soon, Dev

Carson would be a memory. Tearing up his image would hasten that process, if she could just make herself do it. She heard a knock on her office door and looked up.

And her heart stopped.

Dev stood in the doorway looking loose and relaxed in khakis and a work shirt.

She mustered up calm. "Can I help you?" she asked coolly.

He nodded. "Yes. Did you get a chance to look at the signoff sheet I left on your desk?" He walked in to sit in the client chair next to her desk.

He was too close. Having him at eye level made him harder to avoid. "I haven't had a chance to look at it."

"It's just a summary of what's been done. If there are any problems at all, now is the time to write them on the sheet so we can fix them."

"Nice to know you stand behind your work."

"Oh, I do," he assured her. "Anyway, you don't have to do it immediately. Take a day, take a good close look at everything before you give it the okay. Once you're signed off on it, we're gone."

"Great." She set it in her inbox and turned toward her computer. Dev didn't move, though, and in a minute she turned back to him. "Is there something else?"

His expression was watchful. "Yeah, there is."

Don't let him talk about it, she prayed. If he started pawing over the bones of their relationship, she really couldn't handle it. No, she had to handle it, Taylor thought immediately. There simply wasn't any choice.

She folded her hands together to stifle her urge to fidget. "Fine, what do you need?"

"I need to set up a trip," he said.

"Nicole can do that for you," she said smoothly.

"I'd rather you did it." He gave her a winning smile. "It'll just take a minute."

She couldn't think of a dignified way to avoid him, so she finally just stared straight ahead at her computer screen. "Let me just bring up your file from our database." She clicked the keys and then turned to him. "Where would you like to go?"

"Cozumel, of course."

Eyes forward, Taylor thought. Her hands shook only a little. "I see. And will this be for you alone?"

"Nope. I'm tired of vacations on my own. I want to take someone special."

"Two rooms?"

Dev's teeth gleamed. "I said special."

Her face felt frozen. "One room, then."

"Yeah. The honeymoon suite, if they have one."

There was a roaring in her ears. Surely no one, not even Dev, could expect her to get through this. "I see." Taylor brought up her web browser and went to the tour package booking site. "Do you know when you'd like to go?" she asked, typing in her password.

"Let's make it next February. The last week. It'll probably take that long to plan the wedding."

Taylor's hands stilled on the keyboard for an instant before she forced herself to start typing again. "Congratulations," she said tonelessly. She would keep her voice steady if it was the last thing she did, she told herself fiercely. So he'd made up with his fiancée, so what. He wasn't worth having. And if her heart was breaking at the sound of his voice, it was only because she was being foolish. It wasn't like it was a surprise. She'd known he was going back to Melissa. She didn't care. "I'm sure you'll be very happy."

"Thanks, but I haven't asked her yet."

She swallowed. "I'm sure it's just a formality, isn't it?"

He smiled faintly. "Let's hope so," he said, reaching over to pick up the shell in front of her pencil holder.

If she could get through this, she could get through anything, she told herself.

"Does she spell her name the way it sounds?"

"I guess so," he said, toying with the shell. *"T-A-Y-L-O-R..."*

Shock stopped any words she might have spoken in her throat. At last Taylor looked at him, her eyes wide with disbelief. "I think you know how to spell the rest," he said gently.

It was as though she were at the edge of an abyss of uncertainty, of believing, unsure if she were about to fall or fly. "I don't understand," she managed.

"Look, let me tell you about last week." Dev leaned forward. "We'd gotten back from Newport and I was walking around feeling like I didn't fit into my own skin. Something wasn't right but I didn't know what. Then I went into the construction trailer and Melissa was there. And she said something that stopped me in my tracks. She said I was missing something. That's when she came up and put her arms around me, and I knew."

"What?" she whispered.

"That I was in love with you."

Suddenly it was as though she was bathed in heat and light.

"My ex-fiancée, who still remains ex, was never a factor. It's been you since I met you, maybe even since I first saw you. You didn't know that, did you? You're the reason I came here when it was time for the honeymoon." He caught her hand in his.

Taylor just blinked at him.

"Riley was running the project at first and I was on the renovation project at the Peabody," he continued. "I'd stopped in to check something with him and I saw you walk by with Nicole, on your way back from lunch, maybe. You floored me. Melissa and I were fighting like cats and dogs, and here you were, sashaying by in your short skirt, laughing, with that lift to your chin. I was hooked.

"Next thing I knew, I was in the travel agency. I thought afterward that it was probably a good thing that you were busy and I couldn't talk with you, because I didn't know what would have happened. Now I'm just sorry we've wasted time. It's up to you to tell me how much more we have to waste."

"I thought you'd gone back to her," Taylor whispered, leaning toward him.

"We were never together really, not the way you and I are. I love you, Taylor. It's right with us. And whatever I have to do to convince you of that, I will."

She laughed shakily. "It doesn't take much," she said. "That day Melissa called I was trying to figure out how to tell you that I loved you. That was part of why it hit me so hard. I thought I'd just been a fool, once again."

He rose and pressed his lips to hers. "I'll let you

be a fool for me. Because I'll tell you, I'm already a fool for you.''

"It's a deal.'' She grinned. "Now about that trip to Cozumel.''

"Yes?''

"I think March would be much better...''

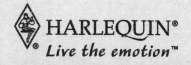

Is your man too good to be true?

Hot, gorgeous AND romantic?
If so, he could be a Harlequin® Blaze™ series cover model!

Our grand-prize winners will receive a trip for two to New York City to shoot the cover of a Blaze novel, and will stay at the luxurious Plaza Hotel. Plus, they'll receive $500 U.S. spending money! The runner-up winners will receive $200 U.S. to spend on a romantic dinner for two.

It's easy to enter!

In 100 words or less, tell us what makes your boyfriend or spouse a true romantic and the perfect candidate for the cover of a Blaze novel, and include in your submission two photos of this potential cover model.

All entries must include the written submission of the contest entrant, two photographs of the model candidate and the Official Entry Form and Publicity Release forms completed in full and signed by both the model candidate and the contest entrant. Harlequin, along with the experts at Elite Model Management, will select a winner.

For photo and complete Contest details, please refer to the Official Rules on the next page. All entries will become the property of Harlequin Enterprises Ltd. and are not returnable.

Please visit www.blazecovermodel.com to download a copy of the Official Entry Form and Publicity Release Form or send a request to one of the addresses below.

Please mail your entry to: **Harlequin Blaze Cover Model Search**

In U.S.A.	In Canada
P.O. Box 9069	P.O. Box 637
Buffalo, NY	Fort Erie, ON
14269-9069	L2A 5X3

No purchase necessary. Contest open to Canadian and U.S. residents who are 18 and over. Void where prohibited. Contest closes September 30, 2003.

◆ HARLEQUIN® *Blaze*™

HBCVRMODEL1

HARLEQUIN BLAZE COVER MODEL SEARCH CONTEST 3569 OFFICIAL RULES
NO PURCHASE NECESSARY TO ENTER

1. To enter, submit two (2) 4" x 6" photographs of a boyfriend or spouse (who must be 18 years of age or older) taken no later than three (3) months from the time of entry: a close-up, waist up, shirtless photograph; and a fully clothed, full-length photograph, then, tell us, in 100 words or fewer, why he should be a Harlequin Blaze cover model and how he is romantic. Your complete "entry" must include: (i) your essay, (ii) the Official Entry Form and Publicity Release Form printed below completed and signed by you (as "Entrant"), (iii) the photographs (with your hand-written name, address and phone number, and your model's name, address and phone number on the back of each photograph), and (iv) the Publicity Release Form and Photograph Representation Form printed below completed and signed by your model (as "Model"), and should be sent via first-class mail to either: Harlequin Blaze Cover Model Search Contest 3569, P.O. Box 9069, Buffalo, NY, 14269-9069, or Harlequin Blaze Cover Model Search Contest 3569, P.O. Box 637, Fort Erie, Ontario L2A 5X3. All submissions must be in English and be received no later than September 30, 2003. Limit: one entry per person, household or organization. **Purchase or acceptance of a product offer does not improve your chances of winning.** All entry requirements must be strictly adhered to for eligibility and to ensure fairness among entries.

2. Ten (10) Finalist submissions (photographs and essays) will be selected by a panel of judges consisting of members of the Harlequin editorial, marketing and public relations staff, as well as a representative from Elite Model Management (Toronto) Inc., based on the following criteria:

Aptness/Appropriateness of submitted photographs for a Harlequin Blaze cover—70%

Originality of Essay—20%

Sincerity of Essay—10%

In the event of a tie, duplicate finalists will be selected. The photographs submitted by finalists will be posted on the Harlequin website no later than November 15, 2003 (at www.blazecovermodel.com), and viewers may vote, in rank order, on their favorite(s) to assist in the panel of judges' final determination of the Grand Prize and Runner-up winning entries based on the above judging criteria. All decisions of the judges are final.

3. All entries become the property of Harlequin Enterprises Ltd. and none will be returned. Any entry may be used for future promotional purposes. Elite Model Management (Toronto) Inc. and/or its partners, subsidiaries and affiliates operating as "Elite Model Management" will have access to all entries including all personal information, and may contact any Entrant and/or Model in its sole discretion for their own business purposes. Harlequin and Elite Model Management (Toronto) Inc. are separate entities with no legal association or partnership whatsoever having no power to bind or obligate the other or create any expressed or implied obligation or responsibility on behalf of the other, such that Harlequin shall not be responsible in any way for any acts or omissions of Elite Model Management (Toronto) Inc. or its partners, subsidiaries and affiliates in connection with the Contest or otherwise and Elite Model Management shall not be responsible in any way for any acts or omissions of Harlequin or its partners, subsidiaries and affiliates in connection with the contest or otherwise.

4. All Entrants and Models must be residents of the U.S. or Canada, be 18 years of age or older, and have no prior criminal convictions. The contest is not open to any Model that is a professional model and/or actor in any capacity at the time of the entry. Contest void wherever prohibited by law; all applicable laws and regulations apply. Any litigation within the Province of Quebec regarding the conduct or organization of a publicity contest may be submitted to the Régie des alcools, des courses et des jeux for a ruling, and any litigation regarding the awarding of a prize may be submitted to the Régie only for the purpose of helping the parties reach a settlement. Employees and immediate family members of Harlequin Enterprises Ltd., D.L. Blair, Inc., Elite Model Management (Toronto) Inc. and their parents, affiliates, subsidiaries and all other agencies, entities and persons connected with the use, marketing or conduct of this Contest are not eligible to enter. Acceptance of any prize offered constitutes permission to use Entrants' and Models' names, essay submissions, photographs or other likenesses for the purposes of advertising, trade, publication and promotion on behalf of Harlequin Enterprises Ltd., its parent, affiliates, subsidiaries, assigns and other authorized entities involved in the judging and promotion of the contest without further compensation to any Entrant or Model, unless prohibited by law.

5. Finalists will be determined no later than October 30, 2003. Prize Winners will be determined no later than January 31, 2004. Grand Prize Winners (consisting of winning Entrant and Model) will be required to sign and return Affidavit of Eligibility/Release of Liability and Model Release forms within thirty (30) days of notification. Non-compliance with this requirement and within the specified time period will result in disqualification and an alternate will be selected. Any prize notification returned as undeliverable will result in the awarding of the prize to an alternate set of winners. All travelers (or parent/legal guardian of a minor) must execute the Affidavit of Eligibility/Release of Liability prior to ticketing and must possess required travel documents (e.g. valid photo ID) where applicable. Travel dates specified by Sponsor but no later than May 30, 2004.

6. Prizes: One (1) Grand Prize—the opportunity for the Model to appear on the cover of a paperback book from the Harlequin Blaze series, and a 3 day/2 night trip for two (Entrant and Model) to New York, NY for the photo shoot of Model which includes round-trip coach air transportation from the commercial airport nearest the winning Entrant's home to New York, NY, (or, in lieu of air transportation, $100 cash payable to Entrant and Model, if the winning Entrant's home is within 250 miles of New York, NY), hotel accommodations (double occupancy) at the Plaza Hotel and $500 cash spending money payable to Entrant and Model, (approximate prize value: $8,000), and one (1) Runner-up Prize of $200 cash payable to Entrant and Model for a romantic dinner for two (approximate prize value: $200). Prizes are valued in U.S. currency. Prizes consist of only those items listed as part of the prize. No substitution of prize(s) permitted by winners. All prizes are awarded jointly to the Entrant and Model of the winning entries, and are not severable - prizes and obligations may not be assigned or transferred. Any change to the Entrant and/or Model of the winning entries will result in disqualification and an alternate will be selected. Taxes on prize are the sole responsibility of winners. Any and all expenses and/or items not specifically described as part of the prize are the sole responsibility of winners. Harlequin Enterprises Ltd. and D.L. Blair, Inc., their parents, affiliates, and subsidiaries are not responsible for errors in printing of Contest entries and/or game pieces. No responsibility is assumed for lost, stolen, late, illegible, incomplete, inaccurate, non-delivered, postage due or misdirected mail or entries. In the event of printing or other errors which may result in unintended prize values or duplication of prizes, all affected game pieces or entries shall be null and void.

7. Winners will be notified by mail. For winners' list (available after March 31, 2004), send a self-addressed, stamped envelope to: Harlequin Blaze Cover Model Search Contest 3569 Winners, P.O. Box 4200, Blair, NE 68009-4200, or refer to the Harlequin website (at www.blazecovermodel.com).

Contest sponsored by Harlequin Enterprises Ltd., P.O. Box 9042, Buffalo, NY 14269-9042.

HBCVRMODEL2

If you enjoyed what you just read,
then we've got an offer you can't resist!

Take 2 bestselling
love stories FREE!

Plus get a FREE surprise gift!

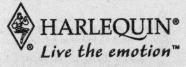

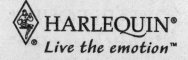